SMALL TOWN PRIDE

SMALL TOWN PRIDE

PHIL STAMPER

HARPER

An Imprint of HarperCollinsPublishers

Library of Congress Control Number: 2021953556
ISBN 978-0-06-311878-2

Typography by David Curtis
22 23 24 25 26   SB   10 9 8 7 6 5 4 3 2 1
❖
First Edition

To my own overly supportive parents.
Mom & Dad, this one's for you.

SMALL TOWN PRIDE

CHAPTER 1

It's all cornfields from this side of the bus.

Empty cornfields. According to my daily planner, it's almost officially spring, but it still feels like winter won't let go. This is by far the worst time of the year: the frost flicks off the grass onto my ankles when I run to the bus in the morning, and even on my way home from school, I have to wear a coat. All that cold, yet there's no snow. No snow *days*. And to top it off, all I get on my bus ride home is this view of dirt.

It's almost time to plant corn, which I know from experience. Well, kind of. See, I spend almost all my downtime playing *Songbird Hollow*, this farming simulation video game where you can do all kinds of things: build farms, fish in rivers, get to know the

1

other townspeople.

You can make friends with the other villagers; you can even fall in love and get married, if that's your thing. And in this game, no one cares who you are, how you act, or what you look like.

But I do it for the farming. In real life, you'd never find me on a tractor, but my farm in *Songbird Hollow* is massive. I've learned a lot about farming from the game, so I know that here in the coming weeks, I'll be able to watch the corn slowly grow outside my bus window, which will finally give me *something* to look at on my ride home that isn't cold dirt.

Something to distract me from the awkwardness waiting for me at home. I wonder if all bus rides will feel like this from now on. Did coming out to my parents really change things forever? Or will this pass? I decide that definitely, probably, it will pass, and then I resume staring out my boring window.

At least if I were on the left side of the bus, I'd see a few cars and trucks drive by, and I'd get the full view of the mayor's house as we pull up to our stop. I have a running bet with Jenna if they'll ever take down their tacky Christmas decorations. But I guess when you're the mayor, you can do whatever you want.

Including seasonally inappropriate decorations.

My mind drifts while I watch the fields turn into woods, and I feel the urge to rest my head on the cool glass. But just as I do, Jenna nudges me in the ribs. I gasp, rubbing the ache as I turn to her.

"What?" I ask.

"Jake!" She throws her hands up into the air. "I just had an entire conversation with you, and you were zoned out the whole time."

"It's not really a conversation if you're the only one talking," I snap, still wincing in pain.

"Don't be rude," she says with a sigh. "Anyway, I was talking *about* you, so that should count."

I smirk, then take in Jenna's gaze. It's almost scary the way she looks at me, so I better do some remembering. I try to recall any of the words she lobbed at me over the last five minutes, but I come up blank. My mind was elsewhere.

There's a hint of concern in her face, and she keeps petting her frizzy blond hair, waiting for a response. When I don't give her one, she rolls her eyes, and her face turns a light shade of pink. I've got to be honest with her about this weekend—and quick.

"I was asking you why your dad's been so weird,"

she says. "I guess I'll do the whole story again. Your dad and I were cutting grass at the same time yesterday—side note: How do you get out of mowing the grass as a weekly chore? It seems unfair. Anyway, so we're cutting the grass, and he stops his riding mower out back where our yards meet. Then he just thanks me. Out of *nowhere*."

"For . . . what?" I laugh. "Did he thank you for accidentally leaving that strip of grass between our driveways uncut, like you do every week?"

Once you get past the first cornfield, the McDonald's, the soy fields, two gas stations, and the second and third cornfields, you'll get to a strip of houses that are a lot closer together. We call it "downtown" Barton Springs. And that's where me and Jenna live, side-by-side neighbors since we were toddlers.

Calling it downtown always feels like a joke, though. It's just a strip of houses flanked by—you guessed it—cornfields. We're on Main Street, the only street that cuts straight through our village.

"You're not funny," she says. "But wait, I actually want to know why you don't have to cut the grass. You have a riding mower. You have no excuse."

"I have grass allergies," I say, but I'm interrupted

by her scoffing. "Fine. I just really hate cutting the grass. Dad makes me do all the laundry every week, and in return, he doesn't make me do outside chores. Anyway, what did he say?"

Being neighbors forever, it's not weird for our families to say hello from time to time, even if that hello devolves into a twenty-minute conversation outside where you start catching up about family, friends, church, weather, and pretty much anything else until one of you says, "Well, I'll let you go"—country code for "OK BYE."

"He just . . . thanked me for being your friend. So, I got all awkward and was like, 'Well, of course I'm Jake's friend. He has a Nintendo Switch and I don't.' Then I had to explain the concept of jokes to your dad. All in all, it was not a great time."

"Oh, well . . ." I say. Here we go. Maybe by talking about it I can figure out how *I* really feel about it. Turning to Jenna, I lower my voice. "I kind of, maybe, came out to them on Saturday?"

"You what? Is that why you were MIA all weekend? We've been planning this for months and you didn't tell me it was happening? I could have been ready with tissues or ice cream or fireworks or *whatever* the occasion called for. How did it go? Are you okay?"

We'd run through dozens of scenarios on how I'd do it. It's kind of been our favorite bus activity lately, but I've always been too cowardly to go through with it. See, I'm out to a whole list of people my age, and they've all been really cool about it. But each time, I felt like I was practicing for this one, ultra-scary moment: telling my family.

I always said I'd tell Mom and Dad whenever it felt right. We'd sit down, I'd confidently break the news to them, and then we'd all hug it out. But . . . months went by and it never felt right. It was easy telling Jenna, sure, but telling my family? I wondered if I'd ever feel ready for that.

But I also knew I was running out of time. Word gets around quickly in this town. Especially when half the school knows, and your mom is the janitor.

"This didn't follow any of our plans," I say. "Believe me. It just came up and I told them. But it went well, I think." My stomach clenches to stop all the uncomfortable feelings rattling around in there. "I still feel a little weird about it, though."

Jenna grabs my hand, and the butterflies in my chest settle, if only for a bit. She's a first-class weirdo, but she's always been there for me. Maybe I should have told her right when it happened, but I couldn't find the words.

"Mom handled it better," I finally say, "but I think Dad was just surprised, big-time. He's cool, though, I mean . . . he voted for Biden."

"Sure?" she says. "But who he votes for doesn't mean he's, like, automatically accepting of it. Or accepting of *you*. Though, if he's out there thanking me for being your friend, he must have come around to it, right?"

This . . . is why I didn't want to talk about it. My parents were good. They said the things they were supposed to. They were supportive!

Still, a part of me wanted *more*. I thought I'd feel like a whole new person: confident, full of pride. It's not like they did anything wrong. But I wanted them to, I don't know, prove to me that this doesn't change anything. Make me feel like my whole family supports me. My whole *village* supports me.

My eyes turn back to the window. How do people in cities, or even in the suburbs, zone out when they need to think? Do the skyscrapers all blend together, the people? There's nothing like staring out at the fields, hoping the answer pops through like summer corn.

"Was he just sad about it?" she asks. "He seemed sad when he thanked me. Not sad about you being gay, I'm sure, but maybe he was sad he didn't know earlier? Did you tell him you told me first? Maybe he's jealous! No . . . that would be weird . . . I mean, you and I have been best friends forever. But as far as grown-up interactions go, it was an eight or nine on the awkward scale."

Then it clicks. He *was* sad. Picture this: It's last Saturday, before family dinner night. I'm doing homework in the living room, Dad's on the recliner dozing in and out after his weekend shift at the factory, and Mom's on the treadmill watching recorded episodes of *Good Morning America,*

Something about this episode got to me. A cute older boy from Houston was on, and he was talking about how he was chosen to be the grand marshal of his city's pride parade. He was seventeen, sure, but compared to all the adults in the studio with him, and the pictures of his whole community supporting him, he just seemed so young. And god, he was so confident. I wondered if he'd ever spent time in the closet, or if he'd ever felt like he didn't belong.

I wondered if I could ever be like him. To hear

the word "pride" and know exactly what that means, what that feels like. To have your whole neighborhood behind you.

All of a sudden, I started crying all over my math homework, and I'm *not* a crying person. Even when it comes to math.

To my classmates, I'd tested coming out in so many ways—directly dropping the words or slipping it into conversation to see if the other person is caught off guard. At this point, I was a pro at it.

And though Jenna and I ran through every scenario, every possibility for telling my parents, when that guy on the TV started talking about what pride meant to him, I realized I wasn't just waiting for the right time . . . I was *hiding* this from my parents, and I didn't want to hide anymore.

And, well, try crying in front of *your* parents and then not explaining why. Yeah, that didn't work. So, I told them. And Dad just kept saying how he wished he knew.

I clear my throat. "He knows our town—"

"Village," she corrects me.

In Ohio, it takes five thousand residents to make a town. Jenna always likes to remind me that Barton

Springs is many things, but with its two thousand residents, it is not a town.

"Right, our *village* is a little backward sometimes." I sigh. "Like those idiotic 'Don't Tread on Me' bumper stickers."

"Oh, or the balls hanging from people's trucks!"

"And don't get me started on the Confederate flags as you go farther back in the farmlands, as if Ohio wasn't literally in the north. But I mean, it's my dad's hometown. He went to our school. My whole family lives within twenty miles of here." I pause for a moment, then say, "Do you think he finally gets that this isn't the most enlightened place for his gay kid to live?"

"I bet that's it," she says, and I think about it.

The bus pulls to a stop. Jenna and I stand to get off at the stop along with the mayor's son, Brett, who's our across-the-street neighbor. I follow Jenna to the front of the bus and give our bus driver, Linda, a quick thank you. When we get off, I bend down to tie my shoe.

"Uhhhhhhhhhh," Jenna starts. "Do you think your dad will . . . I don't know . . . come up with some big gesture to overcompensate?"

"What do you mean?" I ask as I finish tying my shoes.

But when I look up, I see it. Everyone sees it.

I mean, you can probably see it from an airplane.

Some important context here: we have a flagpole in our front yard. It's never really bothered me—we just replace the American flag every few years, try to remember to put it at half-mast when we're supposed to. Nothing big and flashy.

Until today. My eyes lock on the huge, beautiful rainbow flag waving above me as the bus driver eases back onto the road.

Yep, that's overcompensating.

CHAPTER 2

I take in the new flag that's been added, just underneath the American one. For a brief second, pride swells inside me, and I feel hope. Hope that my parents are fully behind me, hope that maybe one day I can be that proud seventeen-year-old, grand marshal of my own pride parade.

I'm brought back to reality, to my backward-acting farming village. Sure, my home might be an accepting place, and my friends have been good about it, and that's amazing. But I remind myself that, especially when it comes to the adults in Barton Springs, there are definitely homophobes out there, and they could be anywhere.

They could be *everywhere*.

"Well, crap," I say to Jenna, still staring at the comically huge flag flapping above me. "I would have been fine with a hug, you know."

All the colors of the progress pride flag stare back at me: red, orange, yellow, green, blue, and purple horizontal stripes with a triangle of white, pink, light blue, brown, and black on the side. It's a huge, beautiful message of acceptance. It's an invitation to me, their gay son, but it's also a challenge to the village.

A weird feeling crawls up my skin, and it makes me want to take a shower to get rid of it. I feel exposed, like I'm standing outside in my underwear or something.

"Are you okay?" Jenna asks.

I don't really know how to respond to that.

"It's a lot," I reply as my parents rush out of the house to greet me.

Against my better judgment, I turn as the bus slips away, and I see how many faces are pressed to the windows. And this point, everyone on that bus has probably heard rumors about me, if I haven't told them myself, but the flag is confirmation. Now they all *know*.

Jenna casually steps in between me and the bus, marking her place as my protector. If I haven't been bullied for it by now, I'm not sure why having a flag would change things. But it's not like homophobes are known for being logical.

When the bus is finally out of view, I look across the street and see Brett Miller standing on the sidewalk, watching the flag flap in the wind.

I turn, hoping Brett gives up on the whole staring thing. Jenna slips away to her house after a light squeeze of my hand. When she greets her dad with a hug, I see him study the flag with a concerned expression. But then I look at the smile on my dad's face. He's so hopeful and eager that it almost makes me want to join in.

"Aw, I wanted to be out here when you first saw it," Dad says, wrapping me up in a hug. "I just raised it about thirty minutes ago. What do you think?"

Honestly? It's equal parts pretty and terrifying.

Pretty terrifying.

"It's . . . big" is all I can mumble. I feel my cheeks get hot, so I add quickly, "My book bag's really heavy today. I just need to, uh, drop it off inside. I'll be back."

I walk, or run—*am I running?*—to the door, and as soon as I'm inside, the comforts of home calm me down a bit. In the living room, I see the box and wrappings that once held the flag in the middle of the floor, with our clothes steamer next to it.

14

I'm so ungrateful.

That's how I feel, that's what I am, and I know it.

I can picture Dad pulling out the flag and carefully steaming it to let the folds release their creases. Thinking about how he's doing this huge thing for his queer kid.

It's nice, what he did. He's saying this is a safe space, that he and Mom accept me for who I am. I guess it's Dad's way of saying all the words he didn't say this weekend.

It's also his way to help me with the problem I clumsily admitted while crying—that I was out to a lot of people, but with each new person I told, I thought I'd feel more confident, but I didn't feel that pride I guess I'm supposed to feel.

I take the stairs two at a time and burst into my room, dropping my bag on the floor. Out of habit, I almost take a seat at my desk to start busting through my homework. (I like to get it out of the way as soon as I get home so I can play *Songbird Hollow* for the rest of the day without my parents bothering me.)

I'm not doing homework right now. I look outside my window and see that Dad's still standing outside, staring up at the flag. The bus is gone, Brett and Jenna are gone; he's all alone.

I should go back. I should talk to him.

I *know* that.

But, for whatever reason, I'm too scared. So, I shut the door, turn on *Songbird Hollow*, and get lost in the only village where I know I can be myself.

"Jake?" Dad asks after knocking lightly on my door.

I'm not sure why he knocks *as* he's opening the door, like he's trying to respect my privacy just as he's violating it. But it doesn't matter, I'm not doing anything.

In-game, about six days have passed since I picked up the controller. Since each day in the game is about ten minutes, I've been hiding up here for an hour.

"Yeah?" I reply. I try to be chill about it, all cool and disconnected, like I didn't bolt from the front yard and shut myself in here for a whole *Songbird Hollow* week.

"Hey, buddy. I just wanted to see if everything's okay. Is . . . ? Was it too much? The flag?"

I shrug. "No."

I'm totally pulling off this chill vibe. He has no idea how much I'm panicking right now. He takes a seat next to me and offers me a concerned look.

Whatever, like I care. Again, I'm chill.

"Oh, wow. You're sweating," he says. "Can we talk about it?"

Fine, maybe I'm not as chill as I thought.

I sigh and pause the game. I don't know how to say what I'm feeling without sounding ungrateful and rude, and that makes me even more flustered. I try to stammer out a response but eventually just say, "I don't know. I don't want to talk. I just want to play my game."

He stares at me for a second longer, and I know I'm going to lose this battle. I usually lose these kinds of battles—my parents are all about talking through our feelings.

"Okay," he says quietly, and I'm flooded with relief. I almost cry, but I'm able to hold it in, just barely. He doesn't leave the room, though. "How's the game? What are you doing? Digging?"

"You really want to know?" I ask, and he nods, so I explain. I can't really talk about my feelings, but I can definitely talk about this game that I've been sucked into for days at a time. "Well, okay. Right now, I'm digging up seashells. There's a special kind of shell that's really rare, so I just have to keep checking different spots until I find them."

"Does it get boring?"

"Not really," I say. "If I get bored, I can do some fishing or farming in the game. I already have twelve gold shells, but I need twenty to—"

I abruptly stop talking. *This* is not something I wanted to talk about.

"To . . . what?" Dad asks.

"You can take the twenty shells to the town's black-smith, and she'll make you a ring."

"Naturally," he says with a laugh. "What do you do with the ring?"

"I . . . well, my character, who also happens to be named Jake . . . can propose to another villager. It's really silly. I told you—"

"Wait, really?" He scrunches his face in confusion. "Seashells, a blacksmith, marriage? I thought this was just a farming game."

"It is, but it's a lot more than that. You get to know the other villagers, and you give them gifts to become better friends with them . . . and you can—I mean, your character can fall in love and stuff."

"So you can propose to any of these characters?" He gestures to the screen.

I don't explain how, technically, you can propose to

18

anyone with a friendship score of eighty and who you've already been in a relationship with for three in-game days. I *do* hesitate, because I get what he really means.

"I can propose to other guys, if that's what you're asking."

"Oh," he says, and a small smile comes across his face. "That's fantastic. We never had games like that when I was a kid. I . . . don't want to get in the way of your proposal, or anything, but can you show me the town? And the people?"

I laugh and stop digging up seashells. I don't really play video games with my dad—I mean, he grew up on, like, Super Nintendo—but he and mom have always been super supportive of my hobby, getting me most of the games I want for my birthdays and holidays.

They've helped me build the only escape I've had from the world out there, so that's why I agree. I move the joystick and maneuver to a small house on the edge of the woods.

"Want to meet my boyfriend?" I ask, and he just laughs.

After Dad leaves, I finish up my digging for the day and browse the *Songbird Hollow* forums in between bouts of math homework. I drop into the "Gold Sea-shell Tips & Tricks" thread to commiserate with the other players who've been digging for the seashells for hours like me.

I reply, talking about how this better be worth it, and get into a quick back-and-forth with a random person. I talk about my plan to propose to Peter, the in-game character I've been courting.

The commenters all flood the thread with their thoughts on my fictional boyfriend, Peter, or about the fun cutscene you get once you propose. Even this brings a smile to my face in the way the real world can't—I feel just as welcome on these forums as I do in the game.

Outside my window, I see the flag flapping in the wind as the sun sets over Barton Springs. And I wonder if, just maybe, I can feel welcome here one day, too.

CHAPTER 3

The next morning, I'm an *entire* jumble of emotions. Like, I got to really talk to my dad about being gay for the first time yesterday. Sure, I was technically talking about the version of Jake in *Songbird Hollow*, but that's still part of me.

Mom knocks on my door and reminds me that today's Pride Day at school. No, not *that* kind of pride. Tonight, there's a basketball game with our rival school, and it'll be hard not to get swept up in the excitement.

We have these "Barton Pride" Days twice during the basketball season—one for our rival game, and another for the last home game of the season. The school gets decked out in Barton Middle colors, the pep band plays throughout the day, and they even bring in the high school mascot for the mandatory pep rally that gets us out of seventh period.

I pull out a few of my obligatory school pride tees, which all say some variation of *Go Barton Bulldogs!* I settle on the new shirt they've been selling at all the games this year. Everyone else will be wearing it, too, but who cares. I look in the mirror and run my fingers through my dark brown hair.

On my red shirt, *WELCOME TO THE DAWG POUND* is written in silver across my chest, and I almost laugh at how intense it all is, but a part of me loves these celebrations. The sea of red and silver in the halls, the excessive high-fives, the building anticipation from all corners of school, the cheap hot dogs at the concessions stand.

On these days, it's like we're all on the same side, fighting for the same cause. Everyone belongs, no matter who they are.

I love it all.

When I look out the window just beyond my dresser, I see the rainbow flag flapping in the wind. It reminds me that even if this day feels like any other, it's not. The vulnerability creeps in my chest again.

"Almost ready?" Mom pops her head in my room.

She's got her hair back into a ponytail, and as she steps into the room, I see she's all decked in red and silver, too, because not even school janitors are exempt from Pride Day. "I have to be in early today. Want a ride? I can take Jenna, too, if she's ready."

I look back to the flag and breathe a sigh of relief. I am proud—of my school *and* of my sexuality. But . . . I don't think I can face a whole bus of kids right now.

Just beyond the flag, I see Brett Miller, the mayor's son, standing across the street. He's definitely staring at the flag as he waits for the bus.

"If you hurry, we can get McDonald's," she adds.

In record time, I'm flying down the stairs with my book bag. I text Jenna a series of panicked texts:

Mom will drive us today

McDonalds

HURRY

Jenna and I sprint out of our houses at the same time and slide into the back seat of Mom's car.

"I had a feeling," Jenna says. "I just knew this would be a McDonald's day. Your mom is a saint." She balls her hands into fists and does a happy dance in her seat. "Ugh, what's his problem?"

I look to Brett, who's still just gazing up at the flag.

"I don't know. He never talks to me anyway."

I say this in part to please Jenna. The two of them have always had this tense rivalry going on, as they're probably the two most ambitious students in our whole class. Every year, they find something new to compete for: In fourth *and* fifth grade, they were the last two standing at the school's spelling bee. Brett won one; Jenna won the other. In sixth grade, Brett placed first in the countywide poetry competition. Last year, Jenna slayed the seventh-grade Math Olympiad. They've turned one-upping each other into a sport.

They haven't found an academic thing to compete over this year, but knowing them, they'll find something before the year's out.

Oblivious to the unspoken rules of "Ignore Brett at all costs when around Jenna," Mom gets into the car and gives him a quick wave as we pull out of our driveway. At least she doesn't offer him a ride.

The way he looks at the flag, though. He's not . . . angry. He's not disgusted, or anything. He looks at it with these big eyes, like how I must've looked after stepping off the bus.

"I feel bad for that kid," Mom says.

24

"Who, Brett? Why?" Jenna asks, a hint of disgust in her voice.

Mom just shakes her head. "Never mind. Forget I said anything."

We go through the drive-through and get breakfast. Mom puts her large coffee in the cup holder and passes back our food. We pull into the school and park in one of the faculty parking spots while Jenna and I finish breakfast.

From the car, I see teachers steadily pour in from the lot. They're all in red and silver, except Mr. Foley, who always antagonizes the school by wearing the rival team's colors on Pride Days. (He *did* go to school there, but mostly, I think he just likes getting a rise out of people.)

We get out of the car, and Mom gives me a quick hug goodbye.

"Thanks, Mrs. Moore," Jenna says after stepping out of the car. "Oh, wait. Do you mind if Jake and I stop by the utility room after sixth period to put on our face paint for the rally?"

"Of course, dear. Jake, hold up for a second." Mom pulls me aside, and Jenna waits dutifully on the sidewalk that leads to the student entrance. "I know you're stressed about the flag, but I'm sure no one will bring it up. And if you want to take it down for any reason, we will. You know how your dad is—he only knows how to show his love in big gestures. It's why I'm always half dreading our anniversary."

She smirks, so I know she's kidding.

"We can keep it up for now." I shrug. "Everyone knows Dad loves to show his activism through huge home decorations, so it's not like the flag says 'Jake is gay!' or something. Even if people ask, I'll be honest about it. Who knows, maybe everyone will be cool with it?"

She nods. "They will. And if they aren't, well, we'll face it together."

But . . . I know that isn't exactly true. Mom's not in my classes, she doesn't ride my bus. My parents can't protect me from everything. I ignore the gnawing fact that, even though I'm out, it doesn't mean I was ready for the whole town to know my business.

I give Mom the biggest, most confident smile I can pull off.

"Let me know if Brett says anything today," she says. "The mayor . . . his mom . . . just isn't very happy about it."

"She can't do anything about it!" Jenna shouts from the sidewalk. I should've known she was eavesdropping. "It's your yard!"

"Thanks, Jenna." Mom blushes and drops her voice to a whisper. "It'll be fine. Just let me know if anyone gives you a hard time, and I'll have the lunch ladies get back at them. We'll see how they like only getting the crusty, burnt parts of the mac and cheese."

Jenna and I step into the school, and we're instantly swept away in a sea of red. Spirits are high, students are high-fiving teachers, and the band surprises everyone by playing the fight song in the middle of the main hall. For Pride Day, we're all united as one.

So . . . why is it that lately, I don't feel like I really belong?

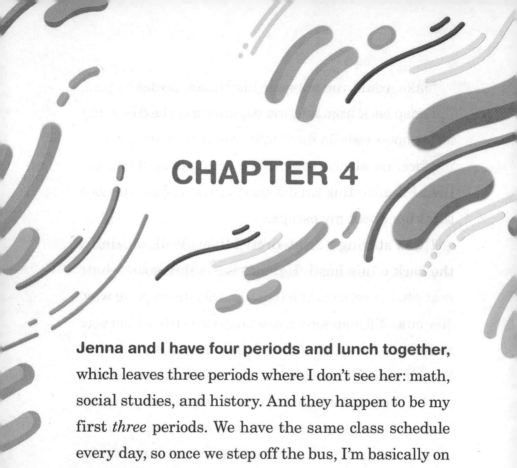

CHAPTER 4

Jenna and I have four periods and lunch together, which leaves three periods where I don't see her: math, social studies, and history. And they happen to be my first *three* periods. We have the same class schedule every day, so once we step off the bus, I'm basically on my own.

Starting every day with math class is, in my opinion, rude as hell. Mr. Foley does nothing to make it better. But he's an okay guy, and he's friends with my mom, so he knows he can't torture me too much.

His teaching is boring, though. I'm lucky I don't fall asleep. I do zone out a lot, and it's like Mr. Foley can sense when my gaze drifts to the door, or to the clock.

"Jake, could you stay on this planet, please?"

I snap back from my first daydream of the day, and I feel people's eyes on me. Embarrassment creeps across my face. He always catches me, then points it out. It's then I realize this time I was not staring at the door thinking about my escape.

I was staring . . . at Brett Miller. Well, officially, the back of his head. He's got this shiny golden hair that always reflects the lights in this distracting way. His buzz cut fades into his tan skin—the Millers go to Florida for all of winter break, and it shows—but he still looks like he has the softest hair in the world.

Mr. Foley passes out a practice worksheet, and my brain is a jumble of decimal points and repeated numbers. Every time I try to focus on it, my mind drifts back to Brett.

Specifically, I wonder *why* I'm looking at him.

It's probably because of his mom. I wonder if he's heard what she thinks about the flag. She has this scary control over the village. Jenna's dad is on the town council, and he always says she puts a lot of pressure on him to vote in her favor on . . . whatever it is town councils vote on. Plus, on the village's website, you can see all her plans for what she calls "Barton Springs's Bright and Clean Future." And she has a *crap ton* of plans.

One thing that doesn't fit her "Bright Future"? Discourse.

A few years ago, she ordered everyone in town to remove their political signs before the last presidential election. Once, I had to go present a project to the town council about a new recycling program to help combat global warming for Earth Day, and she cut me off mid-presentation and moved on to the next agenda topic before I could even finish.

Because of Brett and Jenna's unspoken academic feud, I don't know if he's much like his mom. I decide I should put some extra distance between me and him, just in case.

Eventually, I fill out my math worksheet and turn it in. As the bell rings, Mr. Foley shouts, "Go, Blue Devils," and he's met instantly with boos from me and my other classmates.

Before I can stand from my desk, I hear Ashley's voice booming in my ear.

"Oh my gosh, Jake!" She crouches down, and I pull

back. Her makeup is always on point, but I stare in awe at the highlighter on her cheeks that turns her light brown skin into a shimmery bronze. Ashley's always been friendly to *everyone*, but she usually keeps to her group of girls in the 4-H club.

"Hey, Ash," I say. "What's up?"

She reaches in the front of her book bag, and for a second, I only get a view of her hair—straight black with purple tips. For a farm girl, she's never afraid to make some seriously edgy fashion choices. When she looks back up, she's holding out a little pride flag pin.

"I saw your flag from the bus yesterday, and I wanted to show you this. I got it from Columbus Pride, when I went with my sister, who goes to Ohio State, but I've always felt . . . I don't know, weird about pinning it on my bag." She smiles broadly. "Today that changes. If you can do it, so can I."

She triumphantly pins the pride flag to the front of her book bag and bounds out of the classroom without waiting for me to respond. Which is probably for the best because I'm too caught off guard to say anything coherent. Ashley thinks I have all this pride, but how could I tell her that I'm still unsure, that I really don't?

31

Seeing Ashley's pride pin still gives me a warm feeling in my chest. I take my time packing up and say goodbye to Mr. Foley as I leave.

I head toward my locker to get ready for social studies, but when I get there, I notice someone's blocking it. Someone . . . unexpected. I stop a few paces away and stare at his golden hair to avoid his piercing eyes.

I don't know what to expect.

"Hey, Jake," Brett says. He somehow pulls off this cool, confident pose not unlike the popular kids have, though he doesn't seem to have a ton of friends. "I have to run to English now, but can we talk today?"

"Oh, sure," I say. "Like, on the bus?"

"No," he says. "I don't want people to overhear. It's about the flag. It's . . . important."

Anxiety creeps over me when he mentions the flag. Given everything the mayor's done to keep this village drama-free, I know I have no real reason to trust her son, but a part of me wants to hear him out.

"Sure," I finally say. "Can you come to the utility room before the pep rally? Jenna and I are painting our faces there. *Go, Bulldogs!*"

He grimaces slightly at the mention of Jenna.

"Oh. Well, I wanted to talk to you alone, but sure, Jenna can hear. Do you think she'll be okay with me dropping in on your face painting tradition?" His smile fades. "She doesn't seem to like me very much."

I look away quickly, maybe too quickly, and reach into my locker to swap out my books. Brett and Jenna have always had this unspoken rivalry, but he just spoke about it, which I think breaks the rules.

Although I'm briefly flustered, I have to remind myself that it's Dad's flag he wants to talk about. It's *my* business, and I want to see him, so Jenna will just have to deal.

"It won't be a problem," I say.

Once he leaves, I shut my locker, wondering what this could be about. Mentally, I go through the timeline:

My dad raises this comically huge pride flag in our front yard without running it by literally anyone, including my mom.

The mayor, who famously doesn't take "discourse" very well, is not happy with it.

The mayor's son stops by my locker saying we need to "talk" about the flag.

Is he going to ask me to take it down? Could Mayor

Miller have asked him to talk to me? I want to tell Jenna right now, but we won't see each other until lunch.

Maybe he was looking at the flag this morning out of disgust. Maybe he was just distracted by the pretty colors. Or maybe . . . maybe it's something more.

CHAPTER 5

Later in the school day, the "Barton Bulldogs Pride" starts to die down as all my classmates are bombarded with another day of boring classes—ones that seem even more dull since we know what's coming. School pep rallies are a chance for our basketball team to get hyped up by the whole school, but it's also a warm-up for the cheerleaders, the dance team, the pep band, and, of course, all the students.

The game's not until tonight, so it's kind of a dry run for the evening's festivities. We work on cheers—like my personal favorite, our trademark *Gooooo, Barton Bulldogs! Woof, woof, woof!* It's all a little silly, but it's fun. It's probably stressful for, like, the coach and the players, but for the rest of us, it's just a chance to scream our brains out and think about something that isn't school for once.

After putting our bags in our locker, Jenna and I meet up and walk toward the back of the school. In a small hallway by the band room is the utility room, which doubles as the janitor's office. As we walk in, I take stock of the familiar surroundings: metal shelving with various cleaning products organized neatly in rows, vacuums and floor polishers stored in the back, bags and bags of kitty litter (which Mom uses whenever someone throws up in the cafeteria).

"Hey, y'all," Mom says as we come in. Jenna and I give her a quick hug, but it looks like she's walking out the door. "I'm helping the night shift with trash while the kids are at the rally. Make sure to close this door once you leave. Did you want me to wait around and take you two home today, or will you take the bus?"

"Bus," I say, so she nods and leaves.

"Brett better not be late," Jenna says. "I do not want to miss the band."

"Specifically, the drumline?" I ask. "Even more specifically, the one bass drummer you won't stop talking about?"

"Maybe so, maybe not." She shrugs. "Maybe I just love music, *Jacob.*"

I laugh. "Sure, that's it."

Zack, the bass drummer in question, is cute—I have to give her that—but I'm also pretty sure he doesn't know she exists. Which is hard to pull off when there are only sixty people in our grade. He moved to Barton Springs at the beginning of this school year, which was around the same time Jenna started noticing boys. And she *really* noticed him.

I'd noticed boys a little earlier. But that's another story.

"Last night, I did some Facebook research to see if I could find anyone talking about the flag," Jenna says calmly.

If there's one thing Jenna is fantastic at? It's snooping. She set up a fake boomer account a couple years ago and started friending everyone in town under the alias of Ted Smith from Barton Springs, a name she thought was just generic enough that people would accept the friendship, even if they couldn't place him.

And they did. Last she checked, she had over two hundred Facebook friends from the village. Because of this, she's always got her finger on the pulse of the town's many drama-filled controversies, and we get to see our families' true colors.

But I never thought *I* would be a part of a controversy.

"And?" I ask, ignoring the sinking feeling in my gut.

"Susan Lee, Realtor Extraordinaire, is very supportive. She took a pic of the flag and spewed some vague political jargon, used the hashtag #BartonStrong, the whole works. I didn't even know you could use hashtags on Facebook." She sighs. "Side note: I think the rumors are true. She must be running for mayor."

"Mayor Miller is not going to like that," I say. "I wonder if she knows?"

"She's got to know—I mean, she's up for reelection in November! She must be on the lookout for *any* potential threats. Anyway, there was a lively discussion under the photo. I would show you, but you probably don't want to see all that."

I cringe, but I have to ask. "Did Uncle Jeremy comment?"

She laughs as she unpacks the face paint from her bag.

"Has he ever missed a Facebook post in his life? It's like he lives on there. It's *sad*." The chuckle in her voice fades, and she looks to me. "He wasn't the worst. But

38

he implied your dad was just trying to start drama with the town. They got into it a little bit."

I look down, wondering if I feel better or worse knowing where we stand with my uncle. I haven't told my whole family, and I don't want to. Uncle Jeremy and I used to be so close, but as his and my dad's arguments have gotten larger and more heated, it's clear that, even if he technically lives in Barton Springs, mentally he's on a different planet.

"Thanks for telling me," I finally say.

"You got it. If you ever want to join the fight as our fake boomer man, feel free."

I offer her a smile, and she reaches out to squeeze my hand lightly.

"Um . . . hello?" a faint voice echoes in the dark room.

Jenna grabs my arm and puts a finger to her lips. She pulls me back, hiding in the shadows. When Brett turns a corner into our aisle, she jumps out and screams.

"Whaa!" he shouts, falling backward and knocking into the metal shelves. "Crap, Jenna. Not funny. This place is spooky."

"*Spooky?*" she says with a laugh. "What's spooky, the eight hundred rolls of industrial-sized toilet paper?"

He winces, and his cheeks turn red. "Shut up, Jenna.

And yeah, kind of. It's a *lot* of toilet paper, okay?"

"What's up, Brett?" I ask, stopping their bickering before either of them gets angry for real. They both turn their attention to me.

Jenna pulls a couple face paint sticks from her bag and goes to the sink in the corner of the room. She moistens the sticks, then drags one over her cheek, leaving a clean line of red paint. With the other stick, she accents the line with a shiny silver paint.

"Sorry we had to be so secretive," Brett says. "But I didn't want anyone to overhear."

"Overhear you trying to get Jake to take down his pride flag?" Jenna asks. "That's *so* kind of you."

"Jenna," I warn. Though I can't help but think she might be right here.

She scoffs. "We're onto you, dude."

"What?" Brett asks. "That's not . . . that's not what I'm here for."

"Maybe we should let him explain," I say, but Jenna cuts in.

"Brett, we saw you scheming while looking at the flag this morning. Are you doing this on your own, or did your mom put you up to this? My dad's on the town council and I will—"

40

"Ha! Your dad being on the town council means he's *automatically* siding with my mom." He sneers, but it feels like his anger isn't directed at Jenna. "Anyway, even if Mom asked me to do that, I would've said no."

His eyebrows furrow, and his nostrils flare. Gone is the vulnerable boy who's a little freaked out by the rolls of toilet paper. It's like asking about his mom sets off this fire in him.

"No! Ugh. Let me talk. I think the flag is great, really I do. It reminds me of that time your parents handed out all those Black Lives Matter signs, before my mom snatched up anything she considered 'too divisive' from people's yards. But the flag is like . . . something she can't take away. Unless she climbs up on that flagpole."

She'd really just have to unknot the rope and use the pulley to lower it, but I don't tell him that. A wave of comfort comes over me when he says he supports the flag. Even if it might only be to spite his mother.

A look to Jenna confirms that she doesn't buy his story, so I keep my guard up, too. I give my best poker face. She hands me the paint stick, and I drag it over my cheeks in a few smooth lines.

"Her phone's been ringing constantly since you put

it up, though," he says. "Some people . . . they're angry. They think it sends a bad message to have 'a flag like that' on Main Street. It's the first thing most people see when they enter the village."

I want to say that the first thing people see when entering our village is two cornfields and a McDonald's, but I don't. I *am* feeling a little hurt that Dad's flag is the thing that has the mayor so upset, so I do say, "And what message does it send that the mayor still has Christmas decorations up in March?"

He busts out in a laugh. "Fair point. No one complains about that."

I offer the paint stick to him.

"I don't know how to use this."

"It's easy. Here."

"Is this even allowed?" he asks.

"We follow the *many* face paint rules," I say with a laugh. "Only at approved school events—which includes pep rallies. No full face paint, obviously. Only school colors allowed. Just a pop of red and silver on your cheeks for, you know, school spirit."

He nods, so I dip the paint stick in the running water and hold a paper towel under it to catch any paint drips. I give a slight nod to him, to make sure he's okay with me applying it for him, and he replies with a smile and a nod.

"You just get it wet and rub it on your face basically. But it's super hard to get both cheeks even."

When I go in to add a strip of silver to his cheek, I notice his lips perking up into a half smile. I briefly imagine leaning in and giving him a kiss, and the thought makes me jump back.

"What, is it crooked?" he asks.

"No, no, you look—it looks great. Super even." I hand the sticks back to Jenna, and she starts wrapping them up so we can head to the rally, which should be starting any minute.

I sigh. "Mom said we'd take down the flag if I want. But I don't know what I want. I don't *want* all these people talking about it. I don't want your mom to be angry about it. I just . . . I don't know."

"That's *the mayor's* problem," Jenna says lightly. "I get it, I really do. It's not like I know all the laws here, but something like this can't be, like, against the law. That'd be so unfair. If she's mad, let her be mad. Brett, tell your mom the only message that flag is sending people is that everyone's welcome here."

"I can't tell her anything," Brett says, and I hear

the sadness creep into his voice. "I wanted to tell you because . . . I don't know what Mom's going to do. When I left this morning, she was already talking about involving town council, and you know how they can get."

"You don't have to tell *me* that," Jenna says. "She keeps Dad so busy, his town council job's started to take up more time than his real one."

"I'm sorry. I know what you mean," he says, and for this one brief moment, it's like the tension between Brett and Jenna has eased. "Mom's always been big on her 'vision' for the village, but I think she's extra stressed because she's up for reelection this November. She's been bending over backward to try and make everyone happy."

"Well, that won't make my parents happy, and they vote," I say.

"And there are plenty of people who support the flag," Jenna says, then turns to Brett. "Susan Lee put up this long Facebook post about it, and I saw all kinds of supportive comments."

"Ashley came up to me this morning and told me she supported it, and she even put a little pride flag on her book bag."

Brett uses Jenna's pocket mirror to check out the

paint job. He sighs, then says, "It doesn't really matter how many people support it if they're not the ones who call Mom's office, you know?"

Jenna groans, and I feel more conflicted than I did earlier today. Once we're all packed up, we leave the utility room and walk toward the commotion. The band's playing some old rock medley, and people are already cheering.

The three of us walk into the gym together, and I feel the dynamic change. Being in a two-person friend group is different than this. Even though I wouldn't say I'm really friends with Brett yet, he still made a point to tell me he liked the flag.

I catch a glimpse of his light blue eyes as we walk in, and the sparkle in them makes me blush. It makes me think that, if what he says is true, I made one new ally in all this.

45

CHAPTER 6

We go to find our seats, and Brett follows us. Jenna waves at a couple girls from the softball team before leading us toward them. (Jenna's always had way more friends than I do, but she's always been pretty clear that we're each other's number ones.)

The band goes into the fight song, which means the rally's starting any second now. As we cross under the basketball hoop to go claim the spot near Jenna's other friends, I hear a voice call out to us.

"What is *on* your face?"

The three of us turn—actually, a whole group of students instinctively turn, in a mix of confusion and panic brought on by hearing an adult's scolding voice. That's when the three of us find ourselves face-to-face with Mayor Miller.

"What are you doing here, Mom?" Brett asks.

"Oh god, that's going to take ages to come off," she says as she reaches out to him.

"Actually," I jump in, hoping that'll make her not mess up my (perfect) paint job on Brett's face, "it washes away really easily. Just soap and water. You don't even need to scrub."

"I like it," he says. "You're always saying how I should get into the school spirit more. So, here I am. *Go, Bulldogs!*" he adds.

"Hmm," she says after throwing a suspicious glance to me and Jenna. "Well, we'll see. Clean it off as soon as you get home. Your dermatologist is not going to be pleased. We just got your acne under control."

More classmates turn their heads at the word "acne," like it's a swear word.

"Mom, stop. You're embarrassing me in front of"—he looks to me—"the whole school. I don't like when you do this."

"Ah, another complaint." She shakes her head. "Well, I'll gladly add that to the growing pile on my desk, thanks to—"

"Mrs. Miller!" Jenna shouts as the band finishes the

47

fight song. "So nice to see you, but we've got to grab our seats before they get taken. Jake, *now*."

She pulls me along, and I wait for Brett to follow, but he turns away from us and goes to find a seat across the gym.

So much for our new friendship, I think.

"Told you he was on her side," Jenna says.

Once we take our seats, Mayor Miller launches into a spirited speech about school spirit, but it quickly devolves into a mini campaign event when she talks about the ways she aims to improve the schools should she get reelected. Before she can bore the crowd any longer, she signs off with a quick *Go, Bulldogs!* and exits the building completely.

Once she's gone, our principal welcomes us, and the cheerleaders lead us through the chants.

Goooooooooo, Barton Bulldogs! Go! Fight! Win!

I shout the words and clap along with everyone else, but my heart's not really in it anymore. The mayor is *clearly* annoyed at my family already, and then I went and potentially gave Brett acne again?

B-A-R-T! O! N! I said B-A-R-T! O! N!

I didn't really think that's how acne works, but who knows. He's got a dermatologist, and I don't. But a part of me feels like I just missed an opportunity to make a new friend, and that bums me out.

BAR! TON! BULL! DOGS!

Jenna's caught up with her group of girls and only really leans in to point out when her dreamy crush does something cool with his bass drum. (And it's a big drum strapped to his chest, so there are not many cool things he can do with that.)

Shoot for two! Shoot for two! Shoot for two—OR THREE!

The seventh- and eighth-grade basketball players take the court to excited cheering and shouting from all corners of the gym. It sounds like an arena in here, and I feel my chest swell with excitement. I spot Brett across the gym, but he never looks up. He goes through the motions, sings the fight song with everyone else.

. . . Barton Strong, we show our pride!

"My face is getting itchy," Jenna says as we leave the gym.

I laugh. "Because of all the acne this water-based face paint is giving you?"

We stop at my locker first so I can grab my bag, then walk down to hers. She rambles a bit about our plan for the game tonight, and I keep an eye out for Brett. He's nowhere to be seen—actually, I have no idea where his locker is. But I'll see him on the bus.

We follow the still-chanting crowd out of the school and toward the buses. When I step on the bus, friend groups have shifted. On days when we have basketball games, a group from the baseball team always heads over to Daniel Spencer's house, and they all cluster in the front of the bus. The 4-H girls hang out at Ashley Ortega's farm before coming back to the game in pigtails and red flannel shirts.

Jenna and I, we just have each other.

I slowly pass Brett, waiting for him to look up, but he's staring intently at his phone, listening to some music. He's always like this, a little standoffish, in his own world, but after today it feels personal.

He's already washed the paint off his face, slight splotches of red brush his cheek—from the scrubbing, not from the paint. I didn't think something as basic as face paint would get someone in trouble, but I guess he and his mom have a different relationship than I do with mine.

Before I can think too much about all of it, Jenna pulls me to our seat in the back of the bus. As we sit, she crosses her legs and faces me.

"So, Brett," she says. "Do you think he's planning something? He starts pretending we're friends out of nowhere, then he goes and ignores us right away? Seems shady to me."

I shrug.

"I feel the same way," she says. "There's still a chance he's setting you up for something. Like, gaining your trust so he can eventually get you to give in and take down the flag for Mayor Miller."

"Would he do that?" I ask.

"How many times has he *ever* talked to you before today? And let's not forget, this is the guy who cheated to win that poetry contest."

"He didn't *cheat*," I sigh. "His mom had a friend who published a poetry book and gave him some pointers. That's not cheating."

"Well, when you enter a poetry contest and come in second place behind a guy who knows a semi-famous poet, it sure feels like someone cheated." She shakes her head. "I'm just saying, we don't know enough. He can't be trusted. And you should be careful."

"If he ever wants to talk to me again."

"He's just embarrassed," she says. "His mom kind of

scolded him in front of the whole school. I'd be angry, too. I bet he'll be back, and when he is, you better watch out."

The rest of the ride home is uneventful. Cornfields, woods, then more fields before we finally get to our bus stop. Brett's first off the bus and darts across the street before the driver can even give him the go-ahead. Jenna and I get off after, and she gives me a quick hug before running to her house.

CHAPTER 7

The whole town shows up for tonight's basketball game. And . . . that's not an exaggeration. In the world of eighth-grade basketball, we've got a strong team, and a good shot at making it to the regional playoffs this year.

The stands are a blur of burning, bright red, with little clusters of blue spotted around the visitors' bench. There's a small student section from our rival school, but this is a home game by every stretch of the term. We all cheer, chant, and sing together as basket after basket gets drained.

Jenna clings to my arm with every shot, unless the band's playing; then her attention drifts to Zack the Dreamboat as he beats on what is objectively the most

53

boring drum in the entire band. My other classmates are all around me in the student section, or *THE DAWG POUND* as my somewhat cringy shirt says.

"Have you ever thought about joining the band?" Jenna asks. "It looks like a lot of fun."

I roll my eyes, but she doesn't see—her gaze is fixed on the drumline.

"We don't play any instruments," I finally say.

She just shrugs. "Eh, a technicality."

Brett's nearby, and he's dressed a little too much like the coaches are. He wears a red polo with the Barton Bulldogs logo in silver over his chest, with one of what must be his many pairs of khaki pants. He always has to dress up for something, and I think that's because of the events he goes to with his mom. I wouldn't be surprised if he had some special coaches dinner to go to before this—Mayor Miller is working *hard* for the vote here.

Brett catches my eye for a second, so I give him a light smile and look away before he can break eye contact first.

I look around at all of my neighbors. All the villagers in town. I wonder who here complained to the mayor about the flag in our yard. I wonder who here would be disgusted that I even exist in their midst.

Go, get 'em, Bulldogs! Get 'em OUT! OF! HERE!

I hear what people say sometimes. In the grocery store, at the post office, and all over social media. It's a feeling that nags at me, reminding me that I might never be fully accepted here in my hometown—the one place you'd think would always have your back. Maybe that's why I still don't know what "pride" really means to me, or why I'd rather spend all my free time in a virtual farm town in a video game.

I find myself spiraling in these heavier thoughts until the chanting feels like it's directed at me. It's not team spirit anymore, it sounds like angry shouting.

Go! Go! Go! Get 'em OUT! OF HERE!

Get out of here? But where would I go?

It dawns on me then that I don't want to leave Barton Springs. I mean, maybe I'll go to college away from here, and sure I might change my mind in a few years, but I love it here. I love the farms, our parades, our festivals.

I love the people, even if they don't always love me back.

I guess I just want to belong here. On days when Jenna's dad is stuck at town hall meetings, I'll go to her place and we'll tear through Netflix or Hulu looking for any movies with gay characters. I'll even check out queer books from the library, though we don't have a big selection. So many of these stories make me feel like I should run away to a bigger city like Columbus or Chicago to live my life.

But I think back to *Songbird Hollow* and wonder why I can't have that here. Why can't Barton Springs be the place where I belong? Why can't I just dig up twenty golden seashells and give them to someone and live happily ever after with everyone supporting me?

I barely feel the tears welling in my eyes, but I will *not* cry in front of all of my classmates. Not today, not ever. I pry Jenna's arm off me and shout "Bathroom!" in her ear as I stand up.

"But the game's almost over, and we're tied!"

I scoot past her into the aisle, then sprint down the stairs as to not block anyone's view of the game, before slipping out the closest exit. Immediately, the noise quiets as I turn down the hall.

The concessions stand is closed, even the T-shirt booth is temporarily abandoned as everyone squeezes into the doorway to see the end of the game. I don't know where to go. If I walk farther into the school, I'll get the quiet I need, but I might run into one of the night janitors who will absolutely tell my mom.

The front doors call to me, so I push through them and take a breath of the crisp air. I can still hear the chants, but it's quieter. I'm just in a tee and shorts, which I'm realizing was a big mistake. But I clench my teeth and force myself to tolerate the chilly air. I pass by this group of high school smokers and find a bench on the other side of the lawn.

I can finally breathe.

I don't cry, though. I store those frustrated tears for another day. I hear a sharp cheer from inside, followed by the time-out buzzer. A resentful side of me wants us to lose. Wants my neighbors to be as hurt as I am, even if it's just for a minute.

Looking up from the bench, I see Brett shuffling my way with his arms crossed. He must have followed me out here.

"Jake, how are you not a Popsicle?" he says.

"What are you doing here?" I ask in a not-so-friendly tone, but to be fair he's spent most of the afternoon *and* evening avoiding me.

"I wanted to make sure you were okay." He takes a seat next to me, and I know it's not possible, but it's like I can actually feel his warmth on me like a blanket. "I saw you leave. You looked . . . I don't know. Sad, I guess."

"I *am* sad."

"Why?"

"Your mom," I say. "This village. I just kept looking at all those faces out there, angry and shouting at the game, and I realized any one of them could have called in a complaint about my flag."

I realize that's the first time I've called it *my* flag. Not Dad's flag. Not the flag outside our house.

My flag.

I think, maybe, that's a little bit of what pride is. Taking something like the pride flag and confidently saying: this is a part of who I am. The flag does mean something to me, I realize, and even if I'm still a little scared, I'm a little excited, too.

Neither of us speak for a minute, but it isn't awkward. We hear the muffled cheers from inside, but here it feels quiet and safe. Our breath turns into fog as it comes out of our mouths.

"Do you know why I don't have any friends?" he asks, changing the topic completely.

I laugh. "You have friends."

"Do I?" he replies pointedly. "I eat lunch in between the choir altos and the guys who play fantasy card games. I'm in a few academic clubs and like the people there, but I don't feel like I'm *friends* with anyone. Like you and Jenna? You're inseparable. I so want that kind of friendship, but . . . I don't know. I'm not any good at making friends, and I've learned it's not always easy to be friends with the mayor's son."

I don't know if I can trust his words, but he seems so genuine right now. But what changed? What's different? Mayor Miller is, at best, annoying, and at worst, manipulative. Add that to his never-ending feud with Jenna, and I'm staring at the last person I should want to be friends with.

But . . . there's that part of me that really does want this. And I wonder if it's okay to try and put myself out there. Let him in, just a little bit.

"Maybe we can be friends," I say. "There's no application process or anything, but you could start by sitting near me and Jenna on the bus. Or at the games. There's even an empty desk behind you in Mr. Foley's class, and we could sit next to each other."

"I could," he says, and a rush of embarrassment crashes on me. He said he wants a friendship *like* what me and Jenna have. Not *with* me. That's a clear distinction, and I will be playing this awkward conversation in repeat on my mind for the rest of my life.

"Or you can do that with anyone, I mean." I try to correct. "You probably don't want to hang around me with all the drama my flag's causing your mom."

He laughs. "Actually, I like seeing her so freaked out. Is that bad? She's always trying to be so proper and perfect; she thinks that if she just removes everything people are fighting about, there won't be any more fights and she'll bring harmony to the whole village."

"Harmony . . . and a second term as mayor?"

"Not if Susan Lee has anything to do with it," he says with a smirk. I make a note to tell Jenna she must be right about Susan's upcoming campaign. But then his smirk fades. "All Mom talks about lately is getting enough votes to win. She wasn't like this last time. She was actually really happy campaigning around town. I miss that side of her."

This is probably the time where a friend would assure him it'll be okay. But we're not friends. Not really. I don't know *what* we are, but he did come out to check on me, and that's not nothing.

"You know that old church on Old Barton Springs Road down by that big blue barn?" he asks.

"Ugh, yeah," I say. "Why did they paint it blue?"

"No one knows. For the record, Mom hates that barn, too."

"I'm sure she does."

"But anyway, on the drive up here, Mom was telling Dad about how that pastor called her this morning, ranting away about your flag. It's not funny, it shouldn't be funny, but he seemed so out of touch that even she was laughing about it. He said something like 'Next thing you know, we'll have a whole pride parade in this town, and then what?'"

We laugh at the impossibility of it all. I want this village to be more accepting than anyone else, but I'm not exactly asking for a parade. But still, briefly, I imagine it . . . and it does feel nice.

"He was just a bigot, even Mom knew that."

"What did she say?" I ask. "How did she respond?"

He sighs, and even in the dark, I see his face drop. "She told him not to worry, and that she'd never let 'something like that' happen."

I deflate. So maybe that is Barton Springs, after all. *Go, Bulldogs! Go, homophobia!* I appreciate his honesty, but this talk doesn't make me feel any better. All I want is a hometown I can feel accepted in, but that's never going to happen when there are people like that living here.

I hear the buzzer sound from inside the gym, and a loud cheer makes its way outside of the building. The band plays the fight song.

"Guess we won," Brett says.

"Guess so. Go, Bulldogs." I stand as people start pouring outside. Still cheering, still full of joy. I look out for Jenna, but when the sound of the bass drum reaches my ears, I know she won't leave until the band finishes their set.

"I'm sorry if what I said made you feel bad," he finally says. "I felt bad when I heard it. And . . . it's selfish, I guess, but I needed to tell someone. I needed to tell someone who's like me."

I turn to him, wondering if he just admitted exactly

what I *think* he did, but he won't meet my eyes. He puts his hand on my shoulder, just for a second, and starts walking toward the crowd.

"I hope you feel better," he says. "Bye, Jake."

I blush. "Bye, Brett."

So maybe I can't fully trust him, but that moment? That was real.

CHAPTER 8

The rest of the week goes slowly, after all the excitement of this week's basketball game. Jenna gave me the play-by-play on the way home in the back seat of the car, and it sounded pretty dramatic. Robbie Johnson, our star player, scored a layup for the win just before the buzzer.

Thankfully, my parents didn't press too hard when I said I stepped outside to get a breath of fresh air and missed the end of the game.

On Wednesday, Brett moved to the back of the bus to sit near us, much to Jenna's dismay. He didn't say anything, and Jenna had this habit of keeping her back to him to keep him out of the conversation, but it was a start.

I can't tell if it's just normal Jenna rivalry, or if she's still convinced he's a double agent for his mom (maybe both?), but by the end of the bus ride, she turned to him and asked him what music he was listening to—which seemed like a start.

Today, on Friday, I told Jenna to take the window seat, which earned me a confused look from both Jenna and Brett. But from this seat, it's easy to let Brett into the conversation. When he started talking, I could feel Jenna tense up, but she thawed as soon as he started gossiping about the mayor and the flag. To catch her up, he tells her the story he told me at the basketball game.

"That pastor said *what*?" Jenna nearly shouts. "I wish we *could* have a pride parade, show all those jerks that they can't act like that. You should've said something."

"I just want people to stop complaining." I roll my eyes, then drop my voice. "Brett, your mom stopped by our house yesterday, by the way."

"Wait, what?" he asks.

"Yeah, I could hear her talking to my dad about the flag. She wasn't angry or anything, not like that pastor was. She was actually really nice, saying she personally loved it, but as a mayor, she was concerned about the message it sends to the community."

Jenna scoffs. "What 'message' do all these people think it sends?"

I really wish someone gave me an answer to that, too. But I guess I can't expect them to knock on the door like, *Hey, I'm a huge homophobe, gays are icky, please take down that flag.*

"Anyway, Dad never told me she stopped by. I don't think he knew I overheard. But I wonder if anyone else has talked to my parents about it." I look to Jenna. "Outside of Facebook comments, that is."

After the excitement of sharing secrets with Brett and Jenna this morning, another monotonous day unfolds before me. The teachers all seem to be in good spirits, even Mr. Foley, who's gotten teased mercilessly all week about the last-second Barton win over his high school team.

Later in the day, Jenna and I walk side by side into Ms. Nugent's science class. Known for being an intense, excitable teacher who wears these bright, flashy button-downs every day, Ms. Nugent really is the perfect teacher for sixth period. Though she looks like she came out of a zany kids' book about how "learning is fun!" at least she keeps us awake after lunch. I'm good at science, too, so the combination of a ridiculous teacher with my favorite subject is the best way to fight my usual mid-afternoon drowsiness.

Jenna and I are seated, and she releases a little yelp when Zack walks in the door.

"He's wearing the fire shirt again," she says, pointing to his oversized black button-up shirt with flames that makes his white skin look even paler than usual. He's followed by his best friend, Connor. They're almost as inseparable as me and Jenna.

"The flaaaaaaaames," I say, stretching out the word dramatically. "Your fave."

I'm always a little jealous of his style—Connor's, not Zack-with-the-fire-shirt. He's got a seemingly endless collection of bright tees that look way nicer than the graphic ones I wear. The violet one he wears now seems to pop against his deep brown skin.

A few more classmates pile in just before the bell rings, including Brett, whose assigned seat is behind Zack and Connor. I always feel bad for him, since those two have a habit of tapping drumline songs loudly on their desks until our teacher threatens to separate them.

As class starts, Ms. Nugent reintroduces us to our

final project of the year.

"I've got some big news for everyone," she says. "As you know, your eighth-grade capstone projects include one final presentation: an oral presentation around one theme we've gone over in class this year. Since you've had a few weeks to start doing background research for the topics I assigned to each of you, I hope you've already gotten a start on this, since we have our first draft check-in next week." She pauses for dramatic effect. "But, in case you need any incentive, I was able to secure an incredible prize for best presentation in class."

Out of the corner of my eye, I see Jenna squeeze her pencil tightly. I even feel my heart start to race.

"One eighth-grade student will give their presentation to the Science Teachers of Ohio conference at the science museum in Columbus. And if that doesn't sound glamorous enough, you'll be presented with an award and a two-hundred-dollar gift card to Easton Town Center."

My classmates all start discussing with their friends—I hear some scoffing, some people already deciding what store they'll hit up with their winnings, but then Jenna leans over and says, a little smugly, "Let's see Brett try to take this one from me."

"You'll both have to get through me first," I say, sounding way more confident than I am.

The idea of speaking in front of class kind of freaks me out, so I'm not sure I'd ever want to speak to a whole conference. But, briefly, I can imagine it—the presentation *and* the shopping spree. I know Jenna and Brett are both so confident and focused, but for once, I think I might want the spotlight, too. To give an epic, well-researched speech.

And maybe, along the way, I'll figure out how to actually use my voice.

At the end of the day, I head to the bus and find Jenna's seat empty, which seems odd. As soon as I sit down, Brett launches into a story, so I can't text her to find out where she is. I realize it's actually nice to talk with Brett again, just one-on-one—I love Jenna, but between her rivalry with Brett and her constant scene-stealing, I have to fight to get a word in edgewise.

Eventually, we get to our stop and say our goodbyes.

I hear the flapping of the flag above me as I walk into our house, but I don't look up.

Am I embarrassed by it? No, I don't think so.

But looking at it reminds me of everything. . . . It reminds me of how the mayor stole all those political signs from people's yards. Or like how yesterday Rissa and Jayme—two of the most popular kids in school—stopped their conversation to look at me as I walked past them. Not with disgust, or anything dramatic. But the look was just *off* enough for me to know they're thinking about it, about me.

It reminds me of how I might be building a new, cautious friendship with the son of our biggest enemy. And even worse, it reminds me I still don't know what pride means to me.

Once I get to my room, I don't even pretend to start on homework. It's the weekend, and this week has been the longest of all time. I turn on my game, and instantly I'm sucked into the village of Songbird Hollow.

The *only* village where I'm accepted for who I am.

Yesterday, I took the twenty golden seashells to the blacksmith, and today I get the gold ring. In the game, I dress my character in his usual red-and-black flannel shirt with light jeans and brown boots and go to pick up the ring from Jeanie May, the town's blacksmith. She hands it over, and I go to the little house in the woods where my in-game boyfriend lives.

I know this is a video game. I know it's not real. But there's a weird way that it tugs at my chest every time I initiate a conversation with Peter, the absolutely fictional computer character I'm going to ask to be my country husband.

He's got a chicken coop in the back of his house, and through dialogue over the last few months, he's talked about his favorite chickens, his favorite (fictional) football team, his favorite foods. He doesn't ask me much about myself, but I *guess* that's okay.

A couple weeks ago, to celebrate our relationship rating hitting 90 percent—what the game calls "In Love"—Peter took me on a date. A whole picnic in the town's park. He gave me a kiss even though we were in public, and so many villagers were around but no one cared.

But now it's proposal time. I've been working toward this moment for weeks, and if what everyone says in the forums is true, I'm in for a really sweet cutscene.

In the game, I start a dialogue with Peter and hand over the ring.

The game asks me if I'm sure, and I select YES.

And just like that, I propose to Peter. Fireworks cross the screen, and a cutscene shows me on one knee under a starry night. The other villagers don't ignore us this time: they clap, cheer, and throw this huge spontaneous party for us in the park.

For some reason, that bigot pastor's words echo in my mind, tearing me from my in-game romance.

Next thing you know, we'll have a whole pride parade in this town.

I watch this whole pride festival erupt in Songbird Hollow, in this charming farm village, for me and my video game boyfriend—*fiancé* now I guess. As tears fill my eyes, I think of the *Good Morning America* interview of that older teen being the grand marshal of his town's first pride.

A seed of an idea creeps into my brain.

The logistics bounce in my head, and it seems impossible. Barton Springs is *no* Songbird Hollow, but maybe it could be one day. Maybe, just maybe, we could throw something in this village, something huge and full of joy that for once didn't have to do with a basketball game.

Before I can stop myself, I'm sending a text to Jenna:

Can you meet me on my porch?

Now??

I have an idea . . .

I decide then and there that we can do it. We *will* do it. We're going to throw Barton Springs's first pride.

CHAPTER 9

I texted Jenna after the digital proposal—many times—but she didn't get back to me. On a normal day, this would have annoyed me since we text almost constantly. But on the day of my big breakthrough, each minute feels even longer than the last.

A couple hours after dinner, though, I hear a car pull into Jenna's driveway and sprint down the stairs. When I get outside, I see Jenna, but I don't recognize the car she just came out of. The woman inside the car waves at me as she leaves, and Jenna shuffles my way to meet me on my porch.

"Jenna!" I snap. "I had this whole brilliant revelation, and you ghosted me. Why weren't you on the bus?"

She runs up the steps and takes a seat in the rocking

chair next to mine. As I swing back, she swings front, and we keep pace with each other for a few seconds.

"Where were you?" I ask. "Who was that lady?"

"No one." She clears her throat. "I mean, that was Mrs. Taylor, Connor's mom. It's just a, um, tutoring thing. He needed some help with that presentation in science."

"Connor? As in . . . bass drummer Zack's best friend, Connor?" I ask pointedly.

She looks away distractedly. "Oh, are they friends?"

"Jenna," I say. "You know they are. You stare at the two of them in sixth period every day. You stare at them in the band during every single home game."

"Oh, *right*! He plays the snare drum. I didn't even think about the fact they were friends. Regardless, I can't help it that he needed help with science."

"I don't see you as the type of person who would help someone in an academic competition," I say. "No offense."

"No offense taken." She waves dismissively at me. "Anyway, let's not dwell on that. Tell me this big revelation you had."

Everybody knows Connor is a straight-A student, so I'm not sure why he'd need tutoring from Jenna. But I ultimately decide to let it slip because I have to get this idea off my chest.

"You know how that preacher went on and on about a pride parade to Brett's mom? And everyone thought that was the most ridiculous thing they've heard?" I stop rocking the chair and turn to Jenna. "What if . . . we actually did something like that? Find a way to throw Barton Springs's first-ever pride festival?"

The squeak of her rocking chair slows as she scrunches her eyebrows.

"We could do that," she says. "And really, what's one more festival? We have them like every month in the park. Let's see, there's going to be one for Memorial Day, graduation day, and Independence Day."

"And don't forget the Bologna Festival," I say.

She scoffs. "How could I forget such a proud tradition?"

"Is that too many?" I ask.

"No, that's not my point. I'm saying setting them up should be like clockwork at this point. Dad was just talking about hiring a band for the Memorial Day festival last week, so it's not like their summer is all booked out."

I look up at the flag in my yard, though I can barely make out the colors in the darkness.

"Are you sure you want to play with fire like that?" she asks. "If everyone's flipping out about a flag, what would they say about this?"

"It's scary, but . . . I don't want to let them win. The bigots who are calling the mayor shouldn't be the ones deciding who this town is, you know?"

"I'm with you. And you know your parents will help—your dad loves making big statements, obviously."

"We could really do this," I say, jumping up from the chair with a creak. I start pacing the porch. "But we'll need a lot of help. Can you get intel from your dad on how to throw something like this?"

"I'll see what I can pick up without raising suspicion."

"He's on the town council. We can't do this without him, can we?" I ask.

She shakes her head, then looks down at her hands in her lap.

"I say we get your parents on board first," she eventually says. "Let's keep my dad out of it, at least for now."

"Your dad's not against this, is he?" I ask sharply.

"No, no! Of course not!" she says with a shaky voice. "I think he'd be cool with the festival *as a dad*, but we don't want the mayor to find out until we have a plan, right? If we tell the wrong people, we'd be in trouble.

Love my dad, but he's not the world's best secret keeper."

"Okay," I say. "I think . . . I'm going to text Brett and tell him the plan."

"You're *what*? Are you maybe forgetting who he lives with?"

"He's been our neighbor for about five years now, so believe me, I haven't forgotten." I laugh. "But we have to get him on board. The mayor's got her hands in everyone's business. If we're really going to do something like this, we need to know exactly what she knows at all times."

She sighs. "That's a good point. Start a group message, and add me to it. I don't want you two doing any plotting without . . ."

She drifts off as the sound of high heels on asphalt hits my ears. I look toward the Millers' to see Brett's mom walking down the length of her driveway.

"Hi, Mrs. Miller!" Jenna shouts with a cheesy smile as the mayor walks to the street to collect her mail. The mayor turns and gives us a startled but cheerful wave. As she reaches the mailbox, her gaze flickers to the flag. We stay quiet until she heads back into her house.

As soon as the door closes, I say, "I hope we can

actually keep this a secret."

We talk through a few logistics in whispers.

"So the three of us, and your parents—that's going to be our planning committee?" Jenna observes. "Pretty small."

"Just to start. Once we know what we're doing, Mom can spread the word to a few teachers. Oh! Ashley put that pride pin on her book bag, and she's popular, so I bet she could get a lot of people to help, too."

Jenna furrows her brows. "Maybe Susan Lee will want to be a part of it? That would really fuel her run for mayor, wouldn't it?"

"Maybe? But let's keep her out of it for a while. If we're going to try and get the town council on board, we can't make it sound like politics, you know? We don't want the mayor to find out from her competitor, either."

"Who else, then?" She furrows her brow. "Oh! Maybe once I get the nerve to talk to Zack, he can join!"

"Yeah, definitely," I say, even though I know her getting the courage to even say hi to Zack before June is doubtful.

"All right, I have to get started on my homework," Jenna says as she stands. "Maybe we can have an official planning meeting this weekend?"

"Sounds good," I say as she leaves the porch. When she's gone, I stick around in the rocking chair for a bit, eventually pulling out my phone to draft a message to Brett and Jenna:

Hi Brett! Want to help us plan something really fun and colorful that will definitely make your mom mad?

"No going back once I text him," I say aloud to no one.

I hold my finger over the send button and notice a slight vibration in my hand. I don't know *why* I want him to be on our side so badly, but I know I want him to be a part of this.

I tap send.

When I get back inside, Mom and Dad are sitting in the living room watching some reality show. I ask them to pause it, and take the seat opposite them.

"How's Jenna?" Dad asks.

"She's good," I say. "But we—I—have something to ask you."

Mom turns off the TV completely, sensing the urgency in my voice. Dad gestures for me to continue.

"I know Mayor Miller came here yesterday, to try and get you to take down the flag. I talked to Brett, and she's been getting calls from people who are furious."

Mom and Dad give each other uncomfortable looks.

"I'm sorry you heard that," Dad says. "You don't want us to take it down, do you?"

"Steve, honey, I told him that if he wanted it taken down, we would," Mom replies. "You did this for him, and if it's making him feel singled out or it's putting pressure on him at school, then—"

"Wait," I cut in. "It's not that."

I take a deep breath and wring my hands together.

"Let them be mad," I say. "The flag . . . it's not just for me. I know there are other queer people in this town, whether they're out of the closet or not. And I want them all to feel welcomed here. I want to take it a step further."

"Oh, that's great," Mom says. "How should we do that?"

I smile. "Have you ever been to a pride festival?"

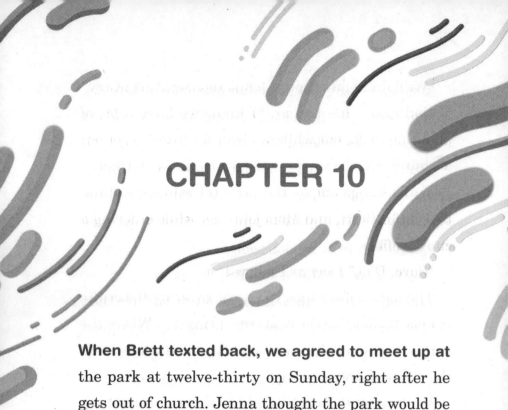

CHAPTER 10

When Brett texted back, we agreed to meet up at the park at twelve-thirty on Sunday, right after he gets out of church. Jenna thought the park would be the perfect location because we needed a quiet place to walk around and plan without people overhearing. Plus, we might want to throw the festival here anyway, so we could start to plan it all out in our minds.

Turns out, neither of us actually thought about how busy parks are on Sundays. It took Mom about ten minutes to find parking in the lot, and as soon as we stepped into the open grass, we found ourselves right in the midst of the Barton Springs Craft Market.

"At least no one could possibly overhear us here," I say, laughing.

"We'll find a quiet spot," Jenna replies, "don't worry."

Dad clears his throat. "I know we have a lot of planning to do, but while we wait for Brett to get out of church, maybe we can take a look at the market?"

Jenna hangs out by the little refreshments stand to wait for Brett, and Mom joins her while ordering a cup of coffee.

"Sure, Dad," I say as I follow him.

The light wind whips the tarps covering the crafts stands. It feels like the first *real* spring day. Where the sun is warm but the wind is cool, and you can smell the grass wherever you go.

We browse the stands, which feature everything from clothing to woodworking projects to cheeses and cured meats.

"Not much produce yet, I suppose," Dad eventually says. "I kind of wanted to pick up some corn."

Without thinking, I laugh. Which just makes him give me a weird look.

"Oh, sorry, Dad. That was rude. It's just that the farmers won't have much to sell until May, and corn won't be ready until the summer. In *Songbird Hollow*, the vegetables I plant in the spring are like . . . artichokes, garlic, fennel, things like that."

"You sure know a lot about vegetables for someone who still needs to be baited with dessert to finish his green beans."

"That's a lie, and you know it!" Heat brushes my cheeks. "I would eat an artichoke right now. I'm, uh, sure they're great. Even if they look a little . . . gross."

"You know, your granny makes the best spinach-and-artichoke dip. Maybe we should grab some of those and ask her for the recipe." He puts a few vegetables into the bag. "How's your game going? Get married lately?"

"Actually, yes."

"You found all those gold seashells!"

I smile. "You remembered! You never remember anything about my games."

He puts an arm around my back. "This one seemed important. So what happened? Was it everything you wanted?"

"It was a little bit of a letdown, actually. There was this big party, fireworks in the park, and everyone was congratulating us in the game. But . . . that's when it really hit me it was just a game." I sigh. "That's why I want to do this so bad. I shouldn't only be able to live my gay life in a video game, you know?"

"I couldn't agree more," he says. "But try not to get engaged anytime soon. You're a little too young."

I roll my eyes. "I don't think you'll have to worry about that."

"One more thing, while we're alone," Dad says, stopping in his tracks. "I want you to know that Uncle Jeremy went on this rant about me and the flag, so I called him."

Chills creep up my spine, and I avoid making eye contact with Dad.

"I think I got through to him, a little bit. I wasn't sure if you wanted me to tell anyone in the family about you, so I didn't say anything directly. But I did tell him he needed to stop treating the flag like it was some personal drama between me and him. We've been fighting so much lately—we were always arguing, but after the last few elections, it became very clear that our differences were bigger than I'd thought."

He sighs. "Did you know I'm not naturally this combative?"

"You . . . could have fooled me," I say.

"But every time Jeremy posts a rant on Facebook, I

thought it was my obligation to match his energy. Kind of combat his weirdo radical views with my own radical acceptance. This flag, though, was always about you."

"Did you at least get through to him?" I ask.

"Who knows, but I tried my best."

"You can tell the rest of the family, by the way. I was so scared to come out to you *because* of the things Uncle Jeremy says, and the way the whole family acts sometimes, but knowing people have my back makes it a whole lot less scary. Is it cowardly not to come out to him myself? Or to Granny?"

He nods. "Jake, whatever makes you feel comfortable, I'm up for it. There's no right or wrong way to come out. I really think they'll all support you in the end, but if I can save you from some awkward conversations, I'll do that."

"Okay, then yes, do that. And thanks for asking me first." I feel the weight being lifted from my shoulders, just slightly. "I don't want things to be awkward when we go to Great-Aunt Bonnie's house for Easter, but I think not telling them would make things more awkward—especially if we get this festival idea off the ground."

By the time we pay for the veggies and make our way

back, Mom's finished her coffee and Brett and Jenna are standing in seemingly awkward silence.

"I think the benches and chess tables down past the market are free," Dad says. "Should we go?"

Mom and Dad talk about the spontaneous veggie purchase while we make our way through the crowded market. Again, I find myself surrounded by people who might be the very people calling in to complain about our flag. Do these people know about me? Why do I care so much?

"Did your mom drop you off?" I ask Brett, but he shakes his head.

"I just took my bike. That's why my hair looks all messy."

I nod, even though it's hard to make a buzz cut look messy. He looks far from messy with his khaki pants and a patterned shirt buttoned to the top.

He must notice me staring, because he says, "Church clothes."

"I've always wondered which church the mayor's family goes to," Jenna says. "It's not one of those mega churches near Akron, right?"

He scoffs. "No, ours is a little more traditional than that. Smaller, too, only about fifty congregants. But it's nice, I kinda grew up with all of them. And of the pastors calling in about your flag, I can promise you ours is not one of them."

"That's nice to know," I say.

"How's your science project going?" Jenna asks bluntly.

"Good, actually. I'm basically done." He shoots her a look, then his expression falls slightly. "Mom and I have done nothing but practice public speaking since."

Jenna releases a sharp grunt as she leads us toward a set of open benches and chairs, but I hang back.

"Are you okay?" I ask Brett.

"Yeah, I'm fine. A little stressed, I guess. Speech prep is really cutting into my *other* homework time, so I haven't gotten a lot of sleep lately. I wasn't even going to tell Mom about the prize, but she has her ways of finding this stuff out."

I reach out to put my arm around his shoulder, but then I wonder if that's weird. So I pull back, and as I do, the fear of his mom finding out about this little meeting starts to stress me out.

"Thank you all for joining"—Jenna turns to my parents—"er, and driving us for the first official meeting of Operation Pride."

"You named it?" I ask, but she just shushes me.

"'What is Operation Pride?' you might be asking." She digs into her backpack and finds printouts from the village website and passes them around.

My cheeks flush as I whisper to Brett, "Looks like someone else has been practicing their speeches, too."

The photos she passes around are familiar. A couple kids having fun on a carousel, fried food and drink stands, an antique car show—all festivals hosted in this very park.

"Right, I'm familiar with this," Dad says in a perky tone. "When I was a teen, your mom and I ran the frozen lemonade stand for every festival."

"Getting paid to sit in a freezer in the middle of July?" Mom sighs dramatically. "Perfection."

I collect the papers and join Jenna. She gives me a nod, and I know I have to take the lead here. I came out on my own terms, but Dad's flag definitely got the word out further than I was ready for. More than anything, I want to control my story. I don't want to be known as the gay kid who kept his pride stored in a flag on his lawn. I want to be known as the kid who brought pride to all of Barton Springs.

"Mom and Dad, we need your help. How can we

throw a pride festival here? A party that looks just like the ones in these photos."

"Except gayer," Jenna adds.

I blush. "Yes, what she said."

There's a silence as they think of what to say. Jenna takes in a breath to speak again—she hates silence—but I grab her hand, just lightly. Our gaze meets, and she nods.

We stand confidently, hand in hand, as the park comes to life around us.

"It wouldn't be easy," Mom says. "But I've been thinking about it, and I think it's doable. Really, we'd just have to get a permit from the town council. They get companies from the area to sponsor all the other festivals, so I'm not sure why they wouldn't do the same for this."

"These town festivals are precious, though." Dad scratches his head. "We're comfortable with this, but I just want to make sure you all know what you might be in for. Brett, with all due respect, your mom is not going to be happy when she hears about this."

"That's kind of the point," Brett chimes in. "She's so focused on her vision of this village—one where we all agree and there's never any controversy, or else—that

90

we really need something like this to shake things up. Let her know that she can't just cater to the homophobes of the world."

"I hate that we even have to talk about this," Mom says, "in the year twenty tw—"

"But we *do* have to talk about it," I interrupt. "I know what some of your friends think. Dad, I've seen some of Uncle Jeremy's Facebook posts."

"You shouldn't have to see that," Dad says with a groan.

"I know it's hard to understand, but I'm not the only gay kid in class," I say. "I'm pretty sure I'm not the only queer person in town. There could be dozens, hundreds even. Statistically, it can't just be me."

I look to Brett, and he offers me a soft smile.

"There are people from all over the county who come to our town's festivals, too," Jenna adds. "This would send a message to everyone who needs it, and it would send an even bigger message to people like Brett's mom."

"You guys, she's not homophobic." Brett says this softly, like he isn't sure his words are true.

"Well, she's certainly not anti-homophobic," Jenna snaps. "She needs to stop listening to all the loud, crusty

91

old people and think about what's best for our village."

I clear my throat and step in before another Jenna-Brett bickering match can begin.

"Jenna, I know we didn't want to involve anyone too close to the mayor, but since Brett's in . . . I think it's time to ask your dad how to file a permit like this. I'll google other small town pride festivals and see how they pulled it off, or if they had any big controversies so we can be prepared for anything." I take a deep breath. "Mom, can you start talking to people in school about it? Just the ones you know will support it. Have them keep it hush-hush for now, but tell them we'll need them to voice their support when the time comes. Dad, we need to get the town on board, and that starts with the whole family. Even Uncle Jeremy."

He hesitates, then nods. "I can't promise anything, but I'll try."

"And, Brett," Jenna adds, making her voice low and serious, "you have the most important job of all: you can't let the mayor find out about this until the time is right. If we have to bring it to town hall, she needs to be totally in the dark."

Brett laughs nervously. "I'll do my best, but you know my mom has ears everywhere."

There's a heaviness that falls over the group as we realize just how impossible this task seems. A pride festival? In *Barton Springs, Ohio*?

"How about we all go to Waffle House?" Mom offers with a smile. "My treat. I want to hear all your ideas. It's going to be a blast once we get this off the ground."

There's no way we can pull this off. But when she stands and wraps me in a half hug, for a moment, I think—maybe we can?

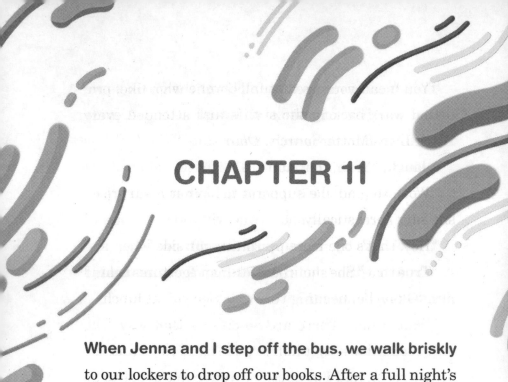

CHAPTER 11

When Jenna and I step off the bus, we walk briskly to our lockers to drop off our books. After a full night's sleep, I'm ready to put our pride festival plan into action.

"Mom should already be spreading the word to the lunch ladies," I say. "Last night, I started looking up all these stories about pride festivals and parades in different small towns."

"Good. We'll want to copy everything they do. And when you see Brett," she says, "I want you to grill him and make sure the mayor hasn't heard anything."

"It's been less than a day," I say. "I know she has ears everywhere, but there's no way, unless Brett went off and told her himself. Oh, and by the way, Dad called my great-aunt Bonnie, and she's in."

"You mean your great-aunt Bonnie who, like, protested wars back in the sixties and attended every Black Lives Matter march in our state?"

I laugh. "Yeah, that aunt."

"Wow, so glad she supports us. What a surprise," she says sarcastically.

"Hey, that's one more person on our side."

"True that." She shuts her locker and gestures behind her. "Okay, I'm heading this way. See you at lunch."

"Wait, what? There are no classes that way. The only rooms down that hall are the band room and the utility room, and I'm guessing you're not about to go hang out with the janitors."

"Well . . ." she starts.

"Ew, don't tell me you're stalking Zack now."

"Oh, please, I'm not *that* desperate. Promise. But you're not the only one with schemes and secrets, and you're going to have to let me have this one for now, mmkay?"

I narrow my eyes at her as we part ways.

As I enter math class, I send a quick wave Mr. Foley's direction. Brett's already there, scribbling furiously in a notebook. I lightly tap him on the shoulder.

"Morning! You okay? You seem stressed."

95

"Yeah, just . . . behind on some homework." He sighs. "Between the basketball game, church, our secret meeting, and the special dinner Mom made us have with Regina and Althea from the town council, I didn't get a chance to finish any of this."

"How much time to do you need?" I ask.

He responds through frantic scribbles. "Five minutes, maybe?"

Mr. Foley always collects homework right at the start of class before morning announcements, and when I look at the clock, I know the bell will ring any second. He doesn't have five minutes. But maybe I can do something.

"Want me to distract him?" I ask.

"Could you?" He looks at me with a pleading expression. He's usually so calm and collected, I've never seen him like this. "Maybe you can ask him about how festival permits work? He always geeks out when he gets to talk about being on the town council, and that could buy me a few more minutes."

"Good idea!"

I jump up from my seat, walk over to Mr. Foley's desk, and take a seat in a chair next to him. He looks up at me with a hint of suspicion—I mean, he must know what Brett is doing. Teachers have that special sense when someone's rushing to do homework right before it's handed in—not to mention, I can hear his pencil scratches from here.

"I have a question," I say, keeping my voice low. "You're on the town council, right?"

"Yessir," he says. "I've been on it for the last few years. Can't say it's a lot of fun, but it's nice to know you're making a difference in the town."

"Huh, sounds like that would be really cool."

He nods. "Hey, maybe you'll be on it one day."

"Maybe," I say. "I was curious, though—if I was trying to get on the agenda for an upcoming meeting, say for an event permit or something, how would that work?"

The bell rings, and after a few dramatic seconds, Mr. Foley says to the class: "I'll collect your weekend assignments after the morning announcements. Since I assume you've double- and triple-checked your work, take this extra time to quadruple-check your answers."

He gives me an odd look. "Right, so. Agenda items. Well, there are a few ways. The easiest way is to come to a meeting and to propose it at the end. They're on the first and third Saturday of the month. We always do an open call for anyone who shows up to raise concerns, complain, propose initiatives, stuff like that. That usually leads us to a . . . spirited debate . . . with all the townspeople."

"Got it, thanks. Just doing some research."

He leans in and drops his voice a bit.

"Oh, and, Jake, I heard about the whole drama with the flag. If anyone gives you a hard time, let me know. I know you can take care of yourself, but I am more than happy to step in."

I smile, and that's when I decide to let him in on the secret. He said it himself: he supports me. We *need* an ally on the town council. And if Jenna won't go to her dad, Mr. Foley might be the next best thing. Sure, his class is a little boring, but he's always looked out for me.

"Fine, I'll be honest," I say, and I hope I'm not making a mistake. "We're going to try and throw a pride festival. With the flag thing, we know the mayor's going to be furious about it, so we're trying to get as much support as possible. Having you on our side when we bring it up to town council would be huge."

"Oh, I . . . see." His expression drops. "I'm sorry, Jake, but I don't think I can help with anything like that."

"Wait, why not?" I ask.

"Jake, I'm sorry, but that's all a little outlandish,

don't you think?" His eyes dart away. "The mayor would never—"

The morning announcements cut him off, but I talk over them. "It's not that outlandish. Smaller towns have done it. More conservative towns have done it. Why can't we?"

"I think it's time for you to take your seat." He looks flustered.

As I turn, the announcements drone on, but I just stew in my disbelief at Mr. Foley. Sure, he works with the mayor, but he's also my mom's friend. I mean, the guy's had dinner at our house before.

Brett puts a hand on my arm, which jolts me out of my thought.

"Thanks, Jake. Just finished, barely. What were you and Mr. Foley talking about?"

"Nothing good," I say under my breath.

Once it's time for lunch, I rush up to my mom, who's just finished mopping part of the cafeteria. Looks like someone already spilled, vomited, or worse, but I'm glad I'm coming at the end of this cleanup.

"Well, good afternoon, honey. How are you doing today?"

I sigh. "Not great. I know I was supposed to leave the teachers to you, but I talked to Mr. Foley about it."

"Oh, not him." She rests her mop against the concrete wall. "Trust me, I know these people. They all love you fiercely and will protect you to the end. But a lot of them don't . . . well, they don't want to rock the boat."

"Oh." My chest deflates.

"Mr. Foley is the trickiest one because we'll actually need him to sign off on this. And I think he will, but he's very logical—he just needs some time for us to show him how we can pull it off."

I help her put a trash bag in the industrial garbage can we have by the tray return area. She continues. "But no more talking to teachers. I've been working at this middle school for ages, which means I know every teacher from fifth to eighth grade. I know the ones who are in the mayor's pocket, I know the ones who are activists. You'd be surprised how much I get to know about these teachers just from sweeping their floors and chatting with them. That new fifth-grade teacher, Mrs. Goin, she keeps a little pride flag in a pen holder on her desk." She pats me on the shoulder. "Just let me handle the politics over here. You go enjoy your lunch."

I keep my mouth shut the rest of the day, and even Jenna seems quieter than usual. I don't want to tell her that I might have spoiled our big secret on day one.

After our last class, she tells me she has to stay late and she'll miss the bus. I don't ask her where she's going, but when she takes a right turn at the end of the hall toward the band wing, I send her a few quick texts.

Wait

Are you going to the band room?

Did you finally talk to Zack or are you just being a creeper???

As I wait for a response, I head to my seat on the bus and wait for Brett to take his spot across from me so we can talk more about our plan.

I can just imagine it now. Mayor Miller and the rest of town council take their seats. They open the floor, and we make our pitch. The audience will be full of all the supporters we can find. Once the town signs off on it, we can get to the fun stuff: raising money, hiring entertainment, buying as many queer flags as we can find.

It'll be just like Songbird Hollow. Bright and colorful and joyful, and maybe I'll even have my hand in someone else's.

Of course, I'm being blindly optimistic, here, but isn't there something in the power of some positive thinking?

"Hey, since Jenna's not here, can I sit with you?" Brett asks, snapping me out of my daydream.

I blush. "Yeah, of course."

When he sits down, a rush of body spray gets swept my direction.

"Is your last class gym?" I ask without thinking.

"Yeah, why? Oh god, do I smell?"

"No! Well, I mean you do, but it's not bad!" I laugh nervously. "It smells like deodorant, I promise. Just, like, a lot of it."

He picks his bag back up and starts to move to the seat across from me.

"No, really, it's okay! Sit with me. We have scheming to do."

Slowly, he takes his seat again and not-so-subtly sniffs the air around him. "Fine, but if I start suffocating you with Axe body spray, you tell me to go."

"It's a deal."

We plot out our attack. There's a town council meeting this weekend, and Brett thinks it'll be best if me and Jenna go up and propose it ourselves—without my parents involved—saying it'll be a lot harder for the council to turn down students.

The smell of his body spray is getting to me, though. It *does* smell good, but also, it's about to make me sneeze. I try to casually pull the collar of my shirt over my nose.

"You can still smell it, can't you?" he asks.

"No," I say, trying to take a shallow breath without coughing.

"God, I'm so sorry." He looks out the window. "Hey, what if we get off the bus at Ashley's stop and walk the rest of the way?"

"That sounds great!" I say, and he throws on his backpack. "Except, will Linda even let us?"

"The fact the bus driver lets you call her by her first name probably means you can get away with it. Here, you ask her."

He pushes me forward as the bus pulls to a stop.

"You zone out, Jake? This is Ashley's house, not yours."

"Hi, Linda! Nope. I just thought maybe Brett and I could be dropped off here and walk the rest of the way."

"You know I'm not allowed to do that," she says. "Not without a note or something."

"Please?" I beg. "Brett and I are working on a project

together, but as you can tell, he smells like an entire boys' locker room, and I can't stand to be in a confined space with him anymore."

She looks behind her. "So that's what that smell is. Fine, go on home, but, Jake, promise me you'll stay in the grass and not the road. I'm going to give your mother a heads-up on the school radio. Brett, honey, next time just spray a little here and here"—she points to each armpit—"and stop before it becomes a shower. The girls only like a little bit, okay?"

"Right," he says as we file out of the bus.

After the bus leaves, he shoves me playfully.

"You could have found another excuse," he says, but then his expression falters as we start walking. "You know what I've started noticing? How literally everyone assumes I'm straight. How everyone assumes *everyone else* is straight."

I nod. "Yeah. Here, it's like you're cis and straight until you say otherwise."

"And sometimes not even then," he says with a touch of sadness in his voice. "I bet that if I told my parents I was bi right now, they'd probably find some way to convince me I wasn't."

"How do you know that?"

"I have a cousin who goes to Miami University, and she came out to all of us at the end of summer break. No one was outwardly rude or homophobic to her for being a lesbian, but you could still tell a lot of people in my family were uncomfortable. We have this big Christmas party every year, and they're always pretty awkward, but this time my aunt kept telling people being gay was so trendy right now, and that she was sure her daughter would grow out of it—like being gay was a weird haircut or something."

I notice his tense pose, his clenched fists. I want to put my hand on his back, but I hesitate. I try to comfort him with my words instead.

"Some people don't get it, I guess. Probably never will." I sigh. "And I'm not sure if you're officially *telling* me anything right now, but if you are, just know . . . I believe you."

"Yeah," he says distractedly before snapping his attention to me. "I am."

"Cool." I smile. "You know, you should come to this pride festival I'm kind of throwing in a few months."

He elbows me in the rib. We both laugh, and the smiles stick to our faces. And we walk the rest of the way home in a kind of happy silence.

"All right, Mom and Dad are leaving me at home as they go to a dinner tonight," Brett says, "so I'm off to do some recon."

"They're not taking you along this time?"

He blushes. "No. I, uh, failed our last social studies test. I haven't had time to study with all of the crap Mom's been making me do, and I can't remember anything from that class without, like, eighty flash cards. I've been screwing up a lot of tests lately. Anyway, Mom convinced Ms. Hardin to let me retake it tomorrow. So I have to stay home and study."

"In that case, recon can wait. I don't want you to—"

"Nope, this is equally important. I'll study *and* pull off a heist." He crosses the street with a devious smile. "All in a night's work!"

CHAPTER 12

After a thoroughly filling dinner of burgers and fries from my favorite fast-food place, Mom and I go our separate ways. She goes to take a bath—the only true cure for a day of being a janitor, according to her—and I go upstairs to work on homework.

But Mr. Foley's math assignments don't seem quite as important right now, not when we could be planning the biggest, greatest party this town has ever seen. But first thing's first: it's time to check on my virtual farm.

I start playing *Songbird Hollow* and take a few minutes to water my plants; then I enter my house. Peter, my in-game husband, has moved in, and he's brought his chicken coops with him. I . . . guess that's how marriage works.

I keep farming in the game, but my skill points are all maxed out. And the only other relationship landmark to come is having a baby, but I definitely don't think I'm ready for that kind of in-game commitment. So for now, I'm just kind of stuck doing the same things and reading the same lines of dialogue.

I put down the game and check out the forums, and I start a new thread to all my fellow *Songbird* friends.

Songbird Hollow Message Boards

Topic: Small town pride

Post from: JakeyJake400

Sorry if this is weird, but I'm just curious if I'm all alone here. So many of you talk about attending big colleges or using this game to de-stress from your busy city careers.

Truth is, I live in a town that's a lot like Songbird Hollow. It's not quite as charming. But we do have a curmudgeonly mayor! And we have farms and farmers markets and festivals, just like in the game.

I proposed to Peter in-game, and I really liked seeing the festival the villagers all threw in the park. They didn't even care that I was a guy, too. It's made me want to throw a festival myself in my tiny village.

A pride festival. Is that weird?

It's going to take a lot of work, but I think we can

do it. Since I'm leading this charge, I don't feel like

I'm allowed to say this . . . but I'm scared.

—Jake

I hit post, then jump as a strange, loud sound comes from outside our house. It's almost like someone dropping pots and pans . . . almost rhythmically? I step out of the bedroom and walk into our spare room, following the noise. When I peek out the window, I can't see much from the darkness, but I hear Jenna's voice.

I run downstairs and slip out the door, and as I come up to her, I'm greeted by the sound of cymbals crashing. I stop when I see two silhouettes on their back deck. A guy's voice sounds out, and I wonder briefly if it could be Zack.

"You've almost got it. Just need to keep them closer to your chest. You'll stay on beat if you don't flail so much."

"I'd stay on beat if I had any sense of rhythm," Jenna replies.

He laughs. As he turns, he spots me in the yard. "Oh, hey, Jake. You want to join the band, too?"

Jenna drops the cymbals with a resounding crash. I plug my ears as I take the steps to the deck.

"Hey, Connor," I say. "What's going on?"

We shake hands, and I feel my gaze linger a little too long on his face. He and I go way back. When we used to go to church, we got thrown into a ton of social events together. Camping, volunteer events, you name it.

But lately, we only see each other in science, and that's from all the way across the room. Now, up close, I can tell he's had a definite growth spurt over the last few months. I notice the top of his lip is dotted with the faintest trace of hair. I'm *immediately* jealous that he's on his way to growing real facial hair.

"Practice is over!" Jenna says. "And look at that, your mom's here to pick you up. Better go out front to meet her. I'll see you tomorrow!"

She pushes him down the stairs as I wave goodbye. I pick up the cymbals and grip them tightly in my hands. They're heavier than I'd imagine.

"Jenna, what's going on?" I ask once she returns. Even in the darkness, I see the red in her cheeks.

She quickly takes each cymbal from me.

"Look. Okay." She releases a dramatic sigh. "Promise me you won't laugh."

"Jenna, you've never once expressed any interest in music as long as I've known you, and I just caught you trying to *secretly* play the cymbals. I'm going to laugh—you know there's no way to be sneaky while playing the cymbals, right?"

"Fine." A smirk comes across her face. "So, during my free period, I may have snuck away to the band room. I had this huge plan of casually bumping into Zack, where I'd casually ask him if he'd like to hang out. And then, bam, we'd be dating within the month."

We take a seat on the ground, and she lightly places each cymbal on top of each other.

"Saying it out loud, it just sounds sad."

"No!" I say, putting my hand on her knee. "I mean, you really like him. You just wanted to say hi."

She shakes her head. "It gets sadder. So, I listened to the end of their practice. It was so fun—it was like I was at a pep rally. That's when I ran into Connor, who was on a bathroom break. I came up with a lie about why I was there, because I definitely wasn't going to tell him I was stalking his best friend."

I look to the cymbals and suck in a breath. "I think I know, but . . . what was the lie?"

"That I wanted to join the drumline. He asked me

what I played, and I said I've always wanted to play cymbals."

"*What?*" I ask, laughing.

"I'm serious! Well, I mean, that was a lie. But I seriously said that! And now Connor is giving me cymbal lessons because he moved up from cymbal to snare this year and he thinks it's perfect timing."

"Oh my god," I say, laughing. "You know you can talk to Zack without joining band, right?"

"I know, I know. I'll talk to Zack soon. But now I need to figure out how to tell Connor I'm not joining anymore." She sighs. "I have been having a little bit of fun, though."

We catch up on our days, and I tell her all about my spontaneous walk home with Brett. I *don't* tell her the secret he told me, of course, but she finally seems to drop the idea that he's our enemy.

"Hopefully Brett's snooping works out for us," Jenna says.

But at that moment, we both get a text from Brett, one that shows us we're sorely mistaken:

Mom knows.

CHAPTER 13

The morning after, I'm still a little shaken. Brett followed up his text with a voice message saying his parents found out he wasn't studying, so they were taking away his phone for the evening.

I haven't spoken with Jenna, but as we parted, I could see she was visibly nervous. The mayor finding out about this early isn't the worst thing that could happen, but it could cause some complications. We just need more information, which is why I can't wait to get on the bus as quickly as possible.

I grab a Pop-Tart as I sprint through the kitchen, book bag slung over my shoulder.

"Bye, Mom! Bye, Dad!" I shout.

"Hold on," Mom says as she comes down the stairs

in her classic janitorial outfit: denim shirt, jeans, and a scrunchie to pull her hair back. "What's the hurry? Bus doesn't come for ten minutes. I was going to see if you wanted to make today our McDonald's day? I'm going in to help the lunch ladies with inventory—and maybe get a few more people on our side—before work."

"Thanks, but I was going to meet Brett and Jenna at the bus stop early."

I start to go, but her denim arm blocks me. "Not without a hug, Jake. And I hate to break it to you, but I saw Brett's mom take him to school about twenty minutes ago. But if Jenna's out there, she can hitch a ride."

We rush to the car, and I flag Jenna down. Did Brett not get his phone back? Is he *grounded*?

"Okay, what's going on?" Jenna says as we climb in the back seat.

"Jenna, you know, the funniest thing happened last night," Mom says.

Jenna wants to talk to me, but she also knows she can't be rude to the person who's about to buy her a McDonald's breakfast. So, she takes a quick breath, then smiles.

"What's that, Mrs. Moore?"

Mom chuckles. "You know, yesterday was a hard day. I rushed to take out all the bags of trash so I could talk to all of my teacher and faculty friends. I was so busy getting support for this pride festival—which, good news, *some* people are psyched about—that I was rushing to throw out the garbage and pulled my back behind the school."

"What? Are you okay?" I ask as Jenna chimes in with "Oh my gosh, I'm so sorry!"

"I'm fine, I'm fine. But this story does have a point. After the longest day I've had in a while, with a twisted back, I got to sink into a nice bath and try out a new bath bomb."

"That . . . sounds really nice, Mrs. Moore." Jenna tosses me a confused look, but I just shrug.

"It was! It was so nice. That is, until I heard the most unusual sound. It was almost like . . . cymbals started crashing outside my window."

I laugh as Jenna covers her mouth. "Oh, that."

"Jenna, what are you doing?" Mom laughs so Jenna knows she isn't really mad. "The school year is about to end. Are you trying out for marching band next year or something?"

"Jenna thinks she's in love with Zack, the bass drummer," I say.

She smacks my arm. "Jake! That's not . . . well, that's not the whole story. It'll all be taken care of soon, I promise. I'll try to keep practicing at Connor's place."

I turn to her. "Oh, you're going to keep practicing?"

"Not for Zack! Really. I'm actually getting the hang of them. Did you know that in marching band, the cymbal players sometimes hold their cymbals out and march alongside the snare drummers, who hit them with drumsticks like they're playing a real drum set? It's kind of cool."

"You can't just join the band in the middle of the year, right?" I ask.

"Maybe not this year. But they have drumline auditions for next year coming up soon, and I think I might actually try."

We're at a stop sign, so Mom turns around in her seat. "Please don't tell me you're doing this all for a boy."

"I'm trying to figure that out," she says, then turns to me. "But you know me, I've got a plan: I just need to hang with Connor more while I figure out how much I like the cymbals, and then, one day, we'll just be hangin' out doing cool percussion stuff, and who else but his best friend, Zack, will walk in the door. We'll hit it off . . . or we won't. And then I have my answer. For band *and* for boys. Easy!"

I start to reply. "Are you sure—"

"I'm supporting you on the pride festival; you support me on this."

My mom clears her throat. "I have to say, I do not miss being in middle school and navigating my first crushes."

"That reminds me, Mom—Brett said the mayor knows about our plan!"

The car goes silent, and Mom's eyes go wide. That makes sense since it's not great news. But then Jenna slowly turns her head toward me with her jaw dropped. I feel like I've said something I shouldn't have.

"Did you hear what you just said?" Jenna asks.

"Brett says the mayor knows about our plan."

Mom chuckles. "Before that."

"Your mom was talking about first crushes, and you said 'That reminds me' before talking about Brett. Don't tell me. You have a crush on Brett? And this is how I find out about it."

"I do not!" My cheeks burn red. "No, no, that's not what I meant!"

"Smooth, Jake," Mom says with a laugh.

When Mom gives our McDonald's order, Jenna leans over and whispers, "Really, though, do you have a crush on him? We don't even know if he's gay."

I do; I know he's bi. But I can't say that to her, and either way, just because we're both queer doesn't mean he likes me.

"I just think he's cute," I say. "I'm not about to join a marching band for him, you know?"

"Please don't," she says with a laugh. "My arms are actually sore right now. From *cymbals*. I promised myself I'd never do an extracurricular again after spraining my ankle in T-ball, and I can't believe I'm about to get wrapped into one because of *lies*."

We pull into the parking lot, and on our way in, Jenna grabs my hand. "Everyone still been good to you since the flag?" she asks. "I know I've been flighty for a bit, but I'll never leave you alone with these wolves."

"Bulldogs," I correct. "Barton Bulldogs, to be specific."

She rolls her eyes.

"People have been good. Ashley's showing her flag pin off to everyone, and even the really popular girls have started going out of their way to say hi to me." I shrug. "I kind of thought there'd be more, I don't know, drama."

"You know, the last time I did my Facebook stalking, there were a lot more people supporting the flag on Susan Lee's post. I don't know if she's deleting any bad messages or if people are tired of fighting, but I feel a little bit of a shift. Don't you?"

"Yeah, I'm actually feeling like people might support this. And support *me*," I say as the warning bell rings. "All right, I'm going to grab my spot in math early so I can talk to Brett."

When I walk into math, Brett's the only other person in the class. He's got his head pressed against his desk, almost like he's sleeping. When I take my seat and put down my bag, gently, I whisper, "Hey, you awake?"

He turns around and gives me a sleepy smile, followed by an exaggerated yawn.

"I have intel," he says, and my heart rate spikes. "Like I said in that text, Mom knows. I snooped on my mom's work computer and found a Word doc with this new legislation she sent out in advance on Saturday's town council meeting."

"Was it bad?"

"It could be. First, it said that all permit requests for events hosted on town property—like our pride festival in the park—must go to a town council vote. This is normal, but it used to be that the mayor could take part in the debate but not vote. But they added a piece that explains that in the event of a tie, the mayor gets to make the decision."

"So essentially . . . the mayor will make every single decision on public events."

He nods. "It's not good. She's got all four of the council members in her back pocket, but even if we got Mr. Foley and Jenna's dad to go against her, she could have the power to cast the deciding vote on this."

"That's unfair!" I say.

"That's not all. I did more digging, and it looks like we were right that any resident could propose a town gathering or festival in the monthly town hall meeting. Basically, we propose it, then we go to a live debate between town council members and townspeople before a final vote is made by the council."

"That's normal, right?"

"Yes, but . . . she's proposing that only Barton Springs residents who are eighteen or older can bring these proposals up in the meeting. To, quote, 'weed out redundant or outlandish requests.' That's new, and honestly, it seems targeted."

Under my breath, I finally say: "Holy crap. You're right. Do you think she knows you're involved, too?"

He shakes his head. "I don't think so. She would have added it to the list of disappointments she threw in my face last night."

He avoids eye contact and starts doodling in the corner of his math homework.

"Hey, are you okay?"

"I don't know," he says. "I barely slept and have no idea how I did on my makeup test. And Mom is pissed because, you know, if I have a bad grade it could hurt her chances at winning reelection."

"She actually said that?" I ask.

"She might as well have." He releases another yawn. "Anyway, I'll try to figure out more. How do you think she found out?"

I let the words sink in while Mr. Foley collects our daily homework. I try to meet his eyes as he stops by my desk, but he won't look up. That's when I realize just how much I screwed up by telling him our plans.

Once he leaves, I whisper, "I think I know who told."

By the time we get to science, the shock of the mayor's changes to the town council still hasn't worn off. In lunch, Jenna promises she'll ask her dad to try to talk to the other members of the council to see if they will break, but I'm not holding my breath. It seems like the mayor has everyone under her thumb.

But maybe we can convince everyone. Maybe we can even convince the mayor herself. We've got to try.

Today, we're all performing the introductory statements of our speeches for the class, as a warm-up for public speaking and a way to get some early feedback about our projects.

We present in alphabetical order, starting off with Zack Bailey. His presentation is called "Periodic Trends of the Elements," and he's not even pretending to care about the families of elements, seems to forget everything he once knew about alkali metals, and keeps stopping abruptly in the middle of his sentences.

I look to Jenna, expecting to see her usual fawning for Dreamboat Zack, but she's cringing along with the rest of us. Jenna's been drawn to his bored, over-it-all attitude, but there's something about it coming up now that doesn't seem to sit right with her, and I'm happy that I have my overambitious friend back.

About halfway through the class, we get to the *M*s, and Brett stands. As he grips his paper, I see his hands shake, just slightly. But once he starts, he wipes the floor with everyone who's gone so far. His presentation—"Acids, Bases, and Neutral Substances on the pH Scale"—is pretty basic, but he's able to explain the topic so clearly that a part of me thinks he'll be a teacher when he grows up.

After he finishes, I curse the fact that our names are so close in the alphabet. I, Jake Moore, have to follow the best presentation of the day. I ease into my presentation on "Using the Half-Life of C-14 to Explain the Appropriate Uses of Carbon Dating." My palms sweat, the paper I'm holding vibrates with my fear, and I can hear my voice getting smaller and smaller.

I'm reading the words off the paper and refuse to look up, and the thought keeps hitting me: How will I ever speak in front of the town council? With that, I'll be so much more vulnerable, I'll be talking about something I really care about, with people in the room who are way more intimidating.

I'm never going to be able to do this.

CHAPTER 14

After school, I jump onto the *Songbird Hollow* forums again and see that I've received a lot of responses to my last post. Some of them are all about small town solidarity, but most of them are saying how "cute" it is that I'm trying to throw a pride in my town.

I clench my fists. I was looking for advice, not for strangers on the internet to be condescending toward me. At least there are no trolls here. In this world, I can come out and be myself, and if people have a problem, they just don't comment. (Even if they did, the moderators would ban them so fast, they'd never see it coming.)

I'm thinking about how I wish some of these commenters were local so we could just make our own

Songbird Hollow, when I see a direct message come into my profile.

I click through:

> Hey! I actually threw my town's first Pride last year, and it was a disaster. We had about twelve people show up, which made it the saddest parade in the world, and by the time we got to the town square, we were nearly outnumbered by protestors.

Anxiety claws at my chest. I don't want to read on, but I know I have to.

> We spent so much time fighting with the town about it. It got so toxic that no company would help sponsor or show up. We realized way too late that we were fighting the wrong fight.

> This year, we split into two teams. One fought with the town, and one spread the word throughout the community—widely! We got support from all over the county, involved local LGBTQ+ school and community groups, we took to every kind of social media.

This year, we already have 3,000 people from all around the area signed up for the event, and that number will just keep piling higher.

If I could pass anything along, it's this: don't fight every small battle. Find as many supporters as you can and go widely with it.

xo—Robert (p.s. I married Peter too—he's the best!)

I call Brett, and he picks up on the first ring.

"Hey, can't talk long. Mom will kill me if she finds out I'm not working on my homework."

"I got a message from someone on the *Songbird* forums who threw their own pride. They said that their first one totally bombed because they were busy dealing with people like your mom."

"What do they suggest?" he asks.

I take a deep, shaky breath. "Going wide with it. Tell everyone, get LGBTQ+ groups on board. Make it such a big thing that your mom can't quiet it down."

"Jake," he says quietly. "There's a process. We can't just . . . wave flags around until people follow us, right?"

"I guess that's true, but if your mom is already using

her power to shut this thing down before it even started, she needs to know there's a lot of support."

He's silent for a minute. "If your parents bring enough supporters to the town hall meeting this weekend, maybe we can convince her. The whole world doesn't have to know."

I don't say that he's sounding a lot like his mom.

I do say: "Fine, maybe you're right. She does need to know that the town wants it. I just need to see if Dad will do the presentation for us."

Brett's anxiety creeps through the phone. "Would he do that for you? Isn't he worried about what the other workers in his factory think? Or his family?"

"Brett, come to your window," I say as I go to mine. He peeks his head out, and I give him a quick wave.

"Does this look like something he'd be scared to do?" I say, gesturing to the giant pride flag in our yard.

"Point made," he says.

"It's not performative, either. At least, I don't think it is." I close the blinds. "I've seen him go in on Uncle Jeremy whenever he shares questionable posts on Facebook. Jenna uses this fake profile to snoop sometimes, and even my uncle's been tame on there lately."

"Good," he says, then adds quickly, "Mom's coming

upstairs. See you at school, Jake."

I smile. "See you."

When I end the call, I see a text pop up on the screen from my older cousin Jessica. She goes to Barton High, and we used to be inseparable, but over the last few years, the feud her dad—Uncle Jeremy—has with mine has kept us apart.

Jake! Why didn't you tell me????

I can't believe I had to find out from my DAD of all people

I laugh as a blush takes over my face. I respond with a quick "Sorry, Jess!" and let her navigate the conversation.

Your flag's a big hit here in the high school!

I mean, there are some jerks but what are you gonna do

Tell me everything! How's everyone at school taking it? Do you have a boyfriend? PLEASE tell me you have a boyfriend!!!

We text back and forth as I get ready for bed—I'd forgotten how much Jess cracks me up. Each time someone new supports me, I feel a little bit more confident. A little bit more like a person who really understands what "pride" means.

But . . . whenever I get the urge to bring up Uncle

Jeremy, I chicken out. I don't know what it is about me that wants his approval. Wants him to see me for who I am and still be there for me like he was when I was a kid. But for now, I can settle for my cousin Jess.

Just know we love you here, ok?

I turn the lights out, pull the blanket over me and smile as I type one last reply:

Love you back.

CHAPTER 15

When I walk into Jenna's house, I'm hit with a musty smell that's so familiar from all our times hanging out. While my parents have made changes to the house over the last few years, hers has stayed the same since her grandma gave it to her dad.

The thick shag carpet, still a bright orange, always feels a little like a massage pad on your feet. Her couches are still in good shape considering they're from the seventies. In every closet, in every corner, they've got reminders of her grandma—old *Reader's Digest* magazines, a stack of records, an old Atari in the basement that probably hasn't been played since Jenna's dad was a toddler.

Jenna greets me with a jump-hug, which is a special

kind of hug more closely resembling a tackle. The first few times she knocked me flat on my butt, but lately I've been able to stay upright.

"Ready to talk business?" she says once I set her down.

"As soon as you are."

She leads me to her dad's office, where it looks like she's just printed a presentation twice as long as the ones they make us do in school.

"I start with goals, so everyone knows what we're there for. But then I dive right into the history of pride parades," she says, handing me the first folder. "That's when you'll unveil all your research on how pride parades have gone for other small towns like ours."

"*We* have to present? I thought Mom and Dad would take care of it because of the new rules."

"It will make more of an impact if we present. Mayor Miller knows it; that must be why she raised the age limit to eighteen. Your dad needs to be there to open the floor, that's all. Then we'll take the stage, answer the questions, and hope for the vote to be in our favor."

I sigh. "And the chances of that happening?"

"Well, I haven't asked Dad outright, but he's obviously

a yes." Her eyes dart away from me as she says it. "The other two on the council, Regina and Althea, are in the mayor's back pocket. They don't have any kids in school with us, and I don't know any other way to convince them. They might be a no, but I *think* we could get one with our speech if the town seems to be on board with it. Mr. Foley is the fourth one, and he's a bit of a wild card."

"He could go either way. He said he'd watch out for me, but that he doesn't support the festival," I say. "But Mom said he responds to logic. I think the presentation will sway him."

She nods, and she starts picking up all the papers scattered around before going back out to the deck. "Well, let's rehearse our parts. We've only got a few days until the next town meeting."

"That means we have two days to make this perfect." I sigh. "We can do it. What about Brett? Should we see if he can come over and rehearse with us?"

She shakes her head. "I've been texting him all day, but I haven't gotten a response. I don't think he's coming."

"Maybe his mom took his phone away from him again. We can talk to him on the bus. He can be our wild card. If Brett proposes it to the town council and there's a split vote, then maybe the mayor would break in our favor?"

"Maybe," Jenna says, but she still won't look me in the eyes.

CHAPTER 16

I hate to sound basic, but taco night is my *favorite* night. Not because of the food (well, not *only* because of the food), but we usually only have it on the random weeknights when Dad is able to work first shift.

He always works second shift at the factory, which means he leaves before I get back from school and comes back around ten, once I'm already in bed. But sometimes they'll need him to fill in the first shift, which is great because we're all up and getting ready in the morning. I don't like having to wait a little longer for the shower, but it's nice to eat Pop-Tarts together over the kitchen sink.

I kind of imagine that's what other families do,

like the ones on TV with parents who have big office jobs. Or even the ones around here lucky to have two parents working first shift, or even one who stays at home.

"Ground beef is ready," Mom says.

"Hard shells are toasted!" I say.

"And the toppings are chopped and ready!" Dad says.

We assemble our tacos, and as soon as we take a seat, my parents try to grill me on homework and my grades.

"Everything's fine," I say. "Look, I wanted to talk to you about the festival."

"Oh, we've talked enough about that lately," Mom says quickly. "We don't want you to be slipping behind on your homework about this."

"Exactly," Dad says with a nod. "We don't need to talk about the festival right now."

I look back and forth, curious why they're avoiding the topic. I mean, we've been talking about it nonstop because it's so important. And now they just clam up and want to talk about *homework*?

"What's going on?" I ask.

There's a long silence that follows, and I can feel

the anxiety building in my chest. I don't know what's going on, but I have a feeling whatever it is is about to ruin taco night.

"Whew, okay." Dad clears his throat. "It's just, it's been hard to get people on board with our plan."

"We keep striking out," Mom says. "The assistant music director? She cornered me in the band room and said she would never support something so evil. And she still goes to our old church!"

"It's not like they actually read the Bible over there," Dad says to break the tension.

But I don't feel like laughing. Hateful people are everywhere, I know that. But couldn't they just shut up for a minute? Why do they always have to have the last say when it comes to celebrating people who are different than them?

"Jake . . . I'm sorry I started all of this. We've been lucky that there hasn't been any vandalism or anything, but while you're at school? People have come by to ask me to take down the flag. People from local government, the local busybodies, some of my coworkers."

"What did you say?" I ask.

"That I want to show LGBTQ+ people in this town that they're welcome here. That one day they'll be comfortable to be who they are."

I blush. "That's sweet."

Mom cuts in. "I said the same thing to the assistant band director, about the festival, and she said there aren't any of 'those people' in our town."

"She knows there are," Dad says. "But sometimes you can't reason with some people."

"Thanks for trying," I say.

"Of course," Dad replies. "And I would tell everyone I have an awesome gay son, but I'm still not sure who all you're telling."

"I know you didn't mean to, but you kind of did that when you raised the flag," I say as Mom's eyes slowly go to his. "I know I told you I was out to a lot of people, but not *everyone*."

He wipes his hand with a napkin, pausing thoughtfully. "I'm sorry. I didn't think about that. You know how I love to put all kinds of social justice signs in the yard. I do it partly to get a rise out of the mayor, but I also do it to, I don't know, combat all the hate out there. If people can wear their hate so proudly on their sleeve, why can't I wear acceptance in the same way?"

"But . . ." Mom starts, and he nods.

"But I was wrong. I should have hung it in your

room until you were ready. Then we could have raised it together."

"Thanks," I say. "I know this is how you show your love or whatever, but it was a lot to take in. I like it now, though."

"Your dad likes to push people's buttons," Mom says, and we laugh.

We eat our tacos in silence for a bit, each of us lost in our own thoughts.

"You know, I was thinking," Dad says. "I could get a bunch of balloons, streamers, flags, and whatever we need and throw a big pride party in the backyard. You can invite anyone you want."

"No!" I say, louder than I meant. "What if I want to push people's buttons, too? I don't want to give up just because a few people aren't happy. I know there are more good people than bad in this town."

There's an awkward silence; then I make my plea:

"The mayor is onto us. She changed local laws so that only people over eighteen can propose new festivals, and she gets to break any ties if the town council is split. At Saturday's town meeting, can you open the floor for us? We can't do this without you. Either of you."

Mom and Dad look at each other and nod.

"We will," Dad says.

"Of course we will," Mom echoes. "And I'm sure it'll all go great."

I just wish they sounded more sure.

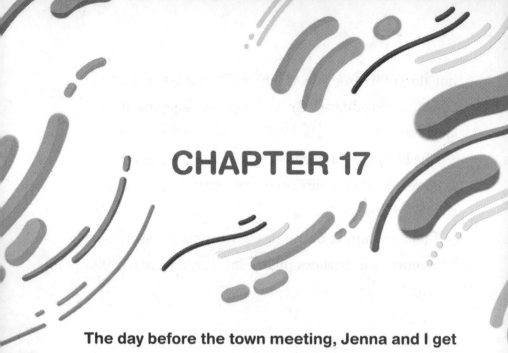

CHAPTER 17

The day before the town meeting, Jenna and I get on the bus and realize Brett is nowhere to be found. His mom must be driving him in today, so I'll have to talk to him about rehearsing the presentation in math class. Before I can comment on it, Jenna launches into a story about her upcoming band audition.

"I have all the crashes down for the fight song, and I even know a few of the drumline marching songs, but I'm still not totally sure *how* to march. Connor says he thinks I'm a shoo-in anyway. There's no marching portion of the audition, since they teach us at band camp. But I'm obviously rhythmically challenged, so I thought I could use the work."

"That's really great," I say. "And no judgment here,

but do you think you might talk to Zack sometime before we graduate? Or are you just keeping it at a slow burn?"

She blushes. "Like you have room to talk! Brett's not even responding to our texts, and look, he's not taking the bus anymore."

I fold my hands in my lap, trying not to let it show how much that bothers me. "I don't even have a crush on him."

"Right."

"I just really like our friendship. It's nice to have a new friend, I guess." She nudges me, and I quickly add, "It's just that you have so many friends—you'd fit in *anywhere*. You walked by the band room once to try and get a boy's attention, and I promise, this time next year you'll be running the whole band."

"I don't have many super-close friends, though, besides you. That's what's been so great about Connor. I hang out with Ashley and the 4-H girls sometimes, but they're not going to invite me to go horse riding or . . . whatever it is they do for fun." She sighs. "You probably remember, but the one piece of advice Mom gave me before she died was to talk to everyone. Be nice to everyone, see who gives that kindness back, and you'll have a wealth of friends to choose from."

"I'm struggling lately with the whole 'be nice to everyone' tip. All these teachers and townspeople who think they're progressive, but crumble the moment they're asked for support."

As we pull into the school lot, she grabs my hand.

"I don't know what to expect from tomorrow's town meeting. But we have to be kind. Let them show their homophobic butts and embarrass themselves."

I nod. "Okay. But if that doesn't work?"

She smiles. "Then we can be a little less kind next time."

I walk into math early, and I see Brett and Mr. Foley in heated conversation at his desk.

"I can't just give you an A, as much as your mom would like." Mr. Foley says.

"Then don't," he almost shouts. "I don't understand some of this stuff, and I can't keep studying all night. Where do I find the time to catch up? We're at a different dinner or event or volunteer opportunity every night. Just give me the C on this. It's not fair you're letting me retake the test multiple times. I didn't do great. I'll try to do better next time."

I take my seat, one ear still firmly pointed toward the conversation.

"I need you to try," Mr. Foley pleads. "I know this is hard, but you're not the only one with a lot of pressure on you. As for where you get the extra time, I've heard rumors you're a part of a certain extracurricular initiative that you might not want to be associated with. And I would hate for your mom to find out about your part in it."

"Those are just rumors," Brett says weakly. "Whatever you're talking about, I'm not a part of it, and you can tell my mom that."

My whole body tenses up when he says that, like we haven't been planning this for a while. *Together.* I grab my backpack, and walk directly out of the room.

Of course, I've never just *left class* before, so I'm freaking out. After surveying my options, I go to the only place I can think of where I can truly hide: the utility closet. Mom takes her time gossiping with the lunch ladies in the morning, so it should be empty.

I start to text Jenna, but on my way to the utility room, I hear the sound of cymbals and laughter from the band room as I pass it. I don't want to mess up whatever's going on there, so I slip into the utility room, and I'm alone.

It all goes down tomorrow.

I think back to the message I got from the *Songbird Hollow* message boards. Unless some miracle happens tomorrow, we're destined for the same ending that happened to their first, failed event.

The door creaks open, and I pull back into the shadows. I'm surrounded by industrial rolls of toilet paper and the mop bucket, so I should be hidden enough. I don't even want my mom seeing me like this.

"Jake? Are you in here?"

I gasp lightly. "Brett?"

I wipe the tears from my eyes as he turns the corner and finds my hiding spot.

"This place is still creepy as heck," he says with a laugh as he sits next to me. "I'm sorry you had to hear that."

"I'm sorry your mom's putting so much pressure on you."

He leans his shoulder into mine, just lightly. Just enough to make me wonder if I imagined it. But it fills me with such a warmth that it must be real.

"Yeah, she's been so much worse since her challenger officially entered the race. Susan Lee."

144

"The town's most famous auctioneer slash Realtor?"

"Mom's furious. Susan Lee's the most famous name in Barton Springs—her name and face are on every For Sale sign in the area already. She won't even have to do much advertising."

My voice drops to a whisper. "I wonder what she'd think of the pride festival."

"You'll see tomorrow, I guess. She should be at the—"

"Don't you mean *we'll* see tomorrow?"

"Jake, I can't join your presentation. As much as I want to get my mom back for all the pressure she's put on me, she really will kill me. And I actually have to study this weekend. If I get another low quiz grade in social studies I'm really screwed."

I cross my arms and nudge his shoulder away from mine.

"I'm also worried that if I go up there and publicly join your cause, they'll think I'm . . . you know. And I'm just not ready for them to find out."

I turn to him. "Then just say you're an ally."

"I can't," he says.

He stands and paces the room. "Don't—you don't know what it's like to have her as a mom. I love my parents, but they're not yours. I'm not ready to come out, and this feels dangerously close to coming out."

"Jenna's straight, and she's still—"

"Jake. I don't feel safe doing it."

I stand, slowly, and walk over to him. I place a hand softly on his shoulder, and he turns toward me.

"I'm sorry," I say. "I was so scared to tell my parents, and I *knew* they'd be cool with it. Your mom's pressuring you enough. I don't want to pressure you, too."

He smiles weakly. "Thank you."

"At least try to come?" I ask, and he agrees.

The bell for second period rings, so we wipe our watery eyes before heading into our next classes.

CHAPTER 18

Dad and I sit on a bench outside town hall, about thirty minutes before the meeting starts. It's a cool night, but the suit and tie I have on has me sweating profusely. Dad's face is bright red, so I bet he's feeling the same way.

Jenna shows up, bringing Connor along with her. He smiles and nods, giving us a hint that he's on our side.

"Are we waiting for Brett?" Jenna asks.

I shake my head. "I don't think he's coming. I'm taking his part in the presentation."

The others look at me cautiously, and Jenna sighs.

"He's siding with his mom, isn't he?"

"No," I snap. "It's more complicated than that."

"We really could have used his voice."

I shrug. "I know, but we can't push him."

"He can help when it comes to planning the big event," Mom says as she lightly paces back and forth. She's got on this nice linen floral button-up, and she keeps flagging down friends and teachers as they pass by.

Once we're allowed in, the searing fluorescent lights remind me of when I was last here, for that school project where the mayor cut me off when we ran out of time.

The board room is moderately sized, with a head table for the council members and the mayor, as well as rows of chairs for all the villagers. We take a seat in folding chairs, but I quickly wish they were beds. The topics they're covering today—park cleanup days, adding a proposed tax levy for the schools to the November ballot, changing lawn clipping pickup day from Tuesday to Wednesday—are all really boring, and my anticipation for the "Open Call" bullet point on the agenda grows and grows.

And then, suddenly, it's our turn.

Jenna and I stand and make our way to the front of the room, but Mayor Miller automatically jumps on the microphone.

"So nice to see you!" she says. "Unfortunately, Open Call items can only be brought forward by residents of

Barton Springs who are eighteen or older."

"Is that a *new* rule?" Susan Lee jumps in with a hint of a smirk in her voice.

"That's okay," Dad says before Mayor Miller can respond. "I'm bringing the item forward. Steven Moore, resident of Barton Springs since 1983. Does that count?"

The gears turn in the mayor's head, but then she says, "Yes, of course. Keep in mind we're running a bit late, so be quick if possible."

The three of us step up to a small podium at the front of the room. It's angled so we get a full view of the mayor, the town council, and all of the townspeople.

My dad makes an introduction, but I can't hear the words. I'm looking at the intimidating, packed crowd. Some hopeful and smiling—like Connor and Susan Lee—some others with a look I can't quite decipher. After his quick comments, Jenna steps up to the microphone.

"Thank you, Mr. Moore. I'm Jenna Thomas, and I wanted to start by giving you a brief history of pride parades and protests."

Jenna uses phrases like "economic revitalization" and I'm not one hundred percent sure what that means, but as I scan the crowd, there is some nodding.

But then I see Uncle Jeremy, who I never expected to be here. I've seen his Facebook posts. I know exactly what he thinks about people like me, the people we're celebrating. A pang of fear hits my stomach, wondering which side of my uncle I'll see today. I remember my cousin's text, saying *Just know we love you here, ok?* And I wonder if I'll get to see how much of that is true today.

Mr. Foley clears his throat, and down the line, the town council members all seem to be getting restless.

And then it's my part.

My palms sweat, and it's just like I felt before my presentation in science. But this is way more important. I feel the adrenaline course through my body, and I put on this fake confidence, hoping that I can push through. I have to do this right.

I take a breath to speak, but my whole body freezes when I see the cute kid in the background. *Brett came!* He must have come with his mom to see the vote. When our eyes meet, he smiles and nods, and I feel the pressure in my chest release. It's the encouragement I need to speak.

"Before we open the floor to comments," I say, "I

wanted to talk about the importance of representation. When LGBTQ+ people of any age see themselves welcomed and celebrated, they're actually much less likely to—"

A man stands in the back, and all the attention swings to him. I vaguely recognize him as one of the basketball players' dads.

"We don't need one of those here," he says. "Maybe it's different in the big cities, but we don't have any of that here."

"And we don't want to invite it," another guy chimes in. I recognize him as a guy who went to school with Dad.

The mayor knocks her gavel, then nods to me. "Let Jake finish."

I appreciate her willingness to hear me out, but I feel my confidence crumbling. My hands tremble. I look down, and my prepared notes are a jumbled mess, in part because I've crinkled the paper, and in part because I'm tearing up.

"That's just not true." My voice cracks, but I push forward. "Just because the queer people here are afraid to be themselves doesn't mean they don't exist."

"Can't this kid move to San Francisco or something?" Dad's old classmate chimes in again, causing some laughs.

It's an out-of-body experience, hearing people say the most cliché . . . things I've ever heard in my life. I can't deny my growing embarrassment, or the hurt that's digging deeply in my chest. But I also feel strangely . . . disconnected. Their reality is so far outside the real world, and they can't blame it on being in a rural town.

I should say something.

I should fight this.

But . . . I can't. I can't find the words. I feel myself closing off completely, looking out into the crowd. The faces that look back at me range from shock to agreement to rage, but knowing there are people are on my side doesn't help.

Brett's hand covers his mouth, but even from all the way back here, I think I see his eyes glisten.

Dad takes the mic. "Dale, do you know why I put up that flag in my yard? It was to support my son, of course, but it was also a message for the whole community. I've heard Mayor Miller ask, dozens of times—what *message* is it sending. The message, Mayor, is that anyone can be safe and loved here. They don't have to hide themselves or take the first flight to New York after graduation." He sighs. "Mayor, *Angela*, we're scaring our children away. And not just those in the LGBTQ+ community. The population here's been dwindling steadily, year over year."

My uncle stands up now, and the other villagers slowly take their seats. I cringe in advance of what he has to say, and I feel the tension from Dad's grip on the microphone.

"My little bro is right." Uncle Jeremy laughs. "Growing up, I used to be so proud of our village for having such a strong bond, but unless we're at a football or basketball game, we're so damn divided. I don't know if I'd attend this here festival—love ya, Jake, but that's not my scene—but it could be other people's. What's the use in stopping it?"

"You're embarrassed of our town now?" Dale asks. "Wait until the paper covers this little—"

Uncle Jeremy grunts. "Don't say something you'll regret."

"Mayor Miller, talk some sense into this group," one of the teachers Mom recruited shouts. "This village welcomes everyone. That's what the website says; that's what *we've* always said. Now do we mean that or not?"

They all argue over top of each other, and words are not minced. I'm feeling dizzy, so I take a seat and feel myself pull my knees up into a ball, just waiting to find out the result of the vote. The last thing I see before I close my eyes is a pale-faced Brett sneaking out the back of the room.

In my mind, I'm in Songbird Hollow, on my fake farm, where none of this happens and I can just be myself.

The mayor raps her gavel three times, and when she rises, it's clear that for all her faults, she is good at commanding a room.

"I think we need some time to think about it. Jake, Jenna, I'd like five copies of that presentation. One for each of the committee members, and one for me. Any residents with feedback on the issue, email or call our office. We'll be back here in one week for the vote."

CHAPTER 19

It's hard to tell if what happened last night was ultimately good or bad. The mayor wanted to see the presentation at least. Jenna and I thought that was maybe a good sign. But I could tell my parents aren't as hopeful.

As soon as I come downstairs for breakfast, my parents' conversation screeches to a halt. Which is always suspicious. I act normal and wander into the kitchen, and their forced smiles are almost laughable.

"Good morning, Jake!" Mom says, but the joy never reaches her eyes.

"What's wrong?" I ask, grabbing a piece of toast from the counter.

Mom and Dad look at each other for a while before

Mom passes me the local newspaper. I unfold it, and the newsprint sticks to my fingers. I realize I'm looking at the backside, so I flip it over.

And I see my face.

"Susan Lee wrote a piece about our petition," Dad says.

I try to read the words, but they all scramble together. I squeeze my eyes shut.

"Don't worry, she paints you in a great light," Mom says. "A group of scrappy tweens against a sitting mayor who's trying to destroy their village's shot at their first pride parade."

"Well, this is great, isn't it?" I say. "She's lighting a fire under Mayor Miller's butt. Just like we did. Right?"

They consider it for a second; then Dad says, "Yes, we lit the fire under her butt, as you so beautifully put it, but we did it to actually support the cause. Call me an old, jaded fool, but I wonder if Susan is doing it for a different reason."

"I bet Susan genuinely believes in the festival and thinks it's a good idea," Mom says. "It's a fantastic story, and it'll get a lot of people on our side, I bet. But . . . there's a political motive there, too."

I shake my head. "So this could be good or bad?"

"Only time will tell," Dad says with a shrug. "It's going to be hard to ignore this article, I'll tell you that."

My phone vibrates about fifty times in a row, so I check my notifications.

Jake please be awake

This is BIG

Connor and I were practicing this morning

And he said we should go get pizza for lunch

THEN I SAID we should invite a couple friends, like I don't know, you and ZACK????

And he was In!

But now you have to be in too otherwise it's going to be a weird third wheel thing for Connor

Not that you'd be dating him, just distracting him

I see the three dots under her name, which means this is not going to end anytime soon, so I just Face-Time her.

"Finally!" Jenna says. The wind's whipping her hair all over the place.

"Where are you?"

"Connor's family's got this huge farm!" she says, but Connor cuts in.

"It's not a farm; it's just a backyard, geez."

"Never mind him. Are you in? Dewey's Pizza, in

about an hour?" She flips her hair out of her face and gives me a pleading face. "Can you ask your mom if she minds driving me back, too?"

I laugh. "We're neighbors. I don't think Mom will mind."

"Mind what?" Mom says from across the room.

I give her a look. "Don't pretend you didn't hear all of that."

"Fine, I was just trying to give you that privacy all you kids seem to care about. Get showered. We'll leave in thirty minutes."

When I get out of the shower, I stand in front of my closet thinking about how rare it is that I'm trying to pick something out that's nice. I mean, we're all playing wingman to set Jenna up on a date with the guy of her dreams—her words, not mine.

When I scan my clothes, I grab a red flannel shirt right away. But then I realize I bought this because it reminded me of my avatar in *Songbird Hollow*. The shirt I—well, he—wore on his first date with Peter.

And I think that maybe I should save this shirt for my first date with a boy, too. I settle on a color-blocked tee that I bought for the new school year and haven't worn since. Usually I just grab whatever Barton Bull-dogs shirt or hoodie I have lying around, so this feels a little special.

We make it to the pizza place right on time. Mom and I get out of the car, while Jenna, Connor, and his mom get out of theirs. We chat briefly while waiting around with Zack.

"I'm Charlotte, Connor's mom. Nice to meet you two."

Charlotte shakes our hands and gives us a sweet smile.

"You know, I heard you caused quite a scene at town hall last night," she said.

"Ah," Mom says. "Read about it in the weekly paper?"

She laughs. "Oh, no, someone from my book club was there, and she was texting the group chat the whole time."

Jenna leans over to me. "She's on our side, by the way. Apparently the book club was split, though."

We go in and get two tables, one for the parents, and one for us—on opposite sides of the room. Jenna knows my mom is cool, but she's not going to want her around for their first kind-of date.

Jenna keeps looking back toward the door, so I try to distract her.

"How's cymbal practice been?" I ask.

Connor answers. "She's a natural. Well, okay, it took her a long time to understand what rhythm was—our fourth-grade music teacher really dropped the ball on teaching her that one. But she eventually picked it up."

"It's a lot harder than I thought," Jenna says, rolling up her sleeves to reveal a bright blue bruise in the shape of a crescent. "I have them on my stomach, too. These things pinch you if you don't watch out."

"Just wait until the high schoolers teach you how to spin them for shows. Their hands are always all cut up. Cymbal playing is basically a sport."

"Do you like doing it?" I ask, kind of bluntly.

Jenna nods. "It's a lot more fun than I thought." When Connor looks confused, she cuts in with "And I thought it was going to be a blast, obviously, which is why I asked you to teach me."

We put in our drink orders, and at this point, Jenna's even stopped turning to stare at the door.

"Sorry, guys," Connor says. "Zack's such a flake.

He's not responding to my texts. Maybe we can just order without him?"

I meet eyes with Jenna, and I'm in awe of how she could so smoothly flip her hair behind her ear, shrug, say it's totally cool, and then start listing which pizza toppings she likes.

I shoot her a quick text saying *sorry*. After reading it, she gives me a sad smile.

But the rest of lunch isn't bad actually. And from the laughter across the restaurant, it seems like Mom and Charlotte are hitting it off, too.

We finish our pizza and get a doggy bag for the couple slices we couldn't finish, which Jenna immediately claims. We regroup with our parents, but as we head out to our cars, Jenna freezes.

Drops her doggy bag on the street.

And I hear her whisper: "Zack."

"Connor! I thought I told you to wait for me. I had to catch a ride with my cousin Logan. Did you have any leftovers at least?"

"Oh!" Jenna says, and drops to the ground to pick up the doggy bag. "Oh, yeah. Here you go."

"Nice." He nods. "Hey, Con, Logan just got the new

Call of Duty. You in?"

Connor turns to Jenna, almost apologetically, but she just waves him on. She knows she's not invited to this kind of hang—and she also knows my mom wouldn't let her jump in a car with a bunch of boys from our grade, especially when they're being driven by Logan, who I assume goes to Barton High.

"Thanks for the pizza!" Zack says, but he says it with half the slice hanging out of his mouth, so it's a little hard to understand.

Once we're in the car, Mom asks, "Who was that guy?"

Jenna's response is monotonous *"That* was Zack. He plays bass drum in the pep band."

"Oh," Mom says. "He seems . . . fun."

Jenna folds her body until her head is against the back of the passenger seat, and her body starts heaving. It isn't until after my initial panic that I see she's laughing. *Hard.*

"He talked while swallowing an entire piece of pizza, right?" she asks. "Like, that wasn't some bonkers nightmare I just had?"

"I'm pretty sure you weren't dreaming," I say.

"I must have been dreaming real hard for the last,

what, six months?" She pulls out her purse and takes her daily planner out of it, revealing *Jenna + Zack* written in different lettering all over. "When I tell you, my heart *hurt* every night thinking of him. I was convinced he was the one."

I shrug. "Maybe he still is? I mean, you don't exactly chew your food, either."

She glares at me. "Don't push this."

When we get home, we take a second to say bye before going to finish our homework for tomorrow.

"Oh my god, Jake," she says. "I just remembered drumline tryouts are *tomorrow*. I don't even know if I want to be in marching band next year. How did this one boy pollute my brain so much?"

I laugh. "You seemed to really like the cymbals. Maybe you should try out anyway? Or, hey, Connor is cute, too—"

"No! I do not make big life decisions for boys anymore. Except for maybe you, but you're special." She puts her arms behind her head and releases a big sigh. "I'll think about it. I did have a lot of fun playing the cymbals. I know I swore off all extracurriculars, but band actually sounds like fun."

"Well. I'm glad the spell got broken. But really, are you okay?"

She shrugs. "I will be. Crushes are just . . . dangerous. You remember that, okay?"

I think of Brett and start to smile.

"No promises."

CHAPTER 20

The local paper that ran Susan Lee's story was not national. It was not regional. It was the *Barton Brief*, the free volunteer press that our township's had going on for decades.

But it's somehow gotten the reach of some huge exposé. Word about the spirited debate at town hall—known more for its bureaucratic snoozefests than shouting matches—reached so far that I'm getting texts from classmates I didn't even realize had my phone number.

Dad's been talking to his family all morning, confirming that they heard the news and that they're all on board to show up for the vote. Mom—who's weaseled her way onto group chats all over the school, from the bus drivers, to the lunch ladies, to the teachers themselves—had to turn her phone off just to get ready in the morning, but plans to spend the rest of the week doing her own campaigning.

As for me? I just need to get to school.

I step onto the bus and instantly lock eyes with Brett. He's smiling, and I slide into the seat next to him.

"No Jenna?" he asks.

"Drumline auditions this morning. Keep your fingers crossed."

He tilts his head. "Still doing this for a boy?"

"I think that crush has . . . crushed. But she still wants to join. I haven't seen Jenna excited about anything like this in a long time, so I hope she makes it."

"Are you going to the basketball game this week?"

"Only if you'll actually sit with me this time. *And* paint your face. We're going all out again."

He gives me a salute. "I'm ready."

The silence that follows is awkward. We both know what went down at the town hall meeting, and he knows I saw him there. He's trying to act normal, but I can't.

"Why did you come?" I ask, looking at my hands, which are folded in my lap. "To the meeting, I mean."

"I guess I just had to see it with my own eyes," he

says. "I'm sorry I couldn't be up there with you. I know it got bad, but I was so proud of you. I don't know how you stayed up there."

I sigh. "I had nowhere to go."

Once we get to school, Brett breaks off to turn in some late homework to Mrs. Nugent, so I walk the halls alone. Everyone knows what happened at this point, and I wonder whose parents were in the room.

There's a sort of silent power in knowing you're getting under your enemies' skins. The homophobia on display feels like a performance. Something they've been programmed to say, a way they've been programmed to feel. And when they get annoyed at the festival and try to blame it on family values or political agendas, it's not much more than a performance for their people. Especially when they're doing the majority of their complaining on Facebook.

As I pass Ashley, she pulls me aside and offers me her pride pin.

"For luck," she says. "For the vote."

I nod, and she puts the pin on the strap of my book bag.

"Thanks, Ash," I say with a smile.

A couple basketball boys slap me on the shoulder in support as I pass them in the halls, and it's around then I wonder: Am I . . . popular? Or do they just love drama?

And, more importantly, if they're just interested in me for the drama I'm bringing to the town, do I care?

I decide then that I don't. Support is support, and for all the crappy things I had to listen to at the meeting, I feel surrounded with love in this school for the first time in a long time. And I did it by being myself.

I always felt like I truly belonged in the very fictional Songbird Hollow, but it's been ages since I felt that way in Barton Springs. But when the town council approves our village's first pride, I'm really going to belong in *my* hometown.

At lunch, I finally get to catch up with Jenna. She's got her food tray resting on a stack of papers, which I'm curious about, but first things first.

"How was the audition?" I ask.

She shrugs. "Good, I think. I should find out soon. This week probably? There weren't a ton of new people. Connor says they don't usually cut people, and it's just a formality, but it was still super intimidating. But I think I crushed it. No, *crash*ed it."

I roll my eyes.

"And the papers?" I say.

"I thought you'd never ask!"

She raises her cafeteria tray and pushes the papers toward me. It looks like a stack of flyers.

"You know those online petitions? I set one of those up for the pride festival, then made flyers to pass around the school so people know where to find the link. Your mom gave me a list of teachers who would be cool hanging them in their classroom."

"Smart," I say. "I'll sign up after we eat."

"I'll put these around the park, too. It's already got thirty signatures!"

I laugh. "That's like half the town!"

"*Village*," she corrects.

We stare at each other for a second.

"This is actually going to work out, isn't it?" I say.

She nods. "You know, I think it will. Susan Lee doesn't miss. No one's heard from the mayor since that article dropped."

▲ ▲ ▲

When I get home, I check on my *Songbird Hollow* farm. My video game husband is right where I left him, sweet and perky (and a little too chicken-obsessed) as always.

I take a virtual walkthrough Songbird Hollow. The farmers markets, the parks, the lakes, the school, the library. The differences between the fictional town and my hometown are becoming smaller and smaller—well, except the fact I don't think we'll ever be getting a blacksmith in Barton Springs.

I check my farms, and just like the fields down the street from us, the corn is starting to grow. Shutting off the game, I climb out my window and walk on the roof to try and see them—something that, officially speaking, I am *never* allowed to do. I lay back on the roof and close my eyes, hearing only the repetitive but calming music of the video game and the flag flapping in the breeze.

The flag that started all this.

"I'm sorry I ever doubted you," I say aloud, and I don't know if I'm talking to the flag or my dad.

I know I can't stay out here long, otherwise I'll get caught, and I do not want to get grounded and miss this week's basketball game. When I come back in, I check the *Songbird* forums and post an update on the pride festival and the big vote that's happening on Saturday. I put on a high-energy playlist and start working on homework with a smile on my face the whole time.

CHAPTER 21

The last few days went by in a blur. The big vote is tomorrow, and our petition has more than two hundred names on it. But that's off everyone's radar tonight because it's the last home game for the Barton Bulldogs basketball team. Excitement is at an all-time high for this game, because if we win, we're in the playoffs.

Brett joins me in the school's utility room so we can paint our faces. He's wearing a red shirt with *WEL-COME TO THE DAWG POUND* on it. With *jeans*. Without the polo shirt and khakis, he no longer looks like a very short coach, and I appreciate that.

"I assume your mom's not coming?" I ask, gesturing at his outfit.

"She's not, so I can wear all the face paint I want."

I turn on the utility room's sink and run one of the face paint sticks under it.

"Sorry for getting you in trouble last time."

"It's fine." He shrugs. "I'm always getting in trouble lately."

"Doesn't that bother you? It seems like your mom's really hard on you. And you're always going to events and dressing up like our teachers."

"When she was first elected, I remember being so excited about it. I don't even remember the last mayor, but she hated him."

"I can't remember him, either. But I do remember when your mom started. I thought it was so cool to live across the street from the mayor."

Drawing the paint stick across my cheek, I make a long, thick silver line. I draw a smaller red line underneath it.

"She really cares about the town. I know that." Brett sighs. "I mean, it's because of her that we have the farmers market on the weekends. She kept driving past these farms that would have old signs saying 'eggs for sale' or small veggie stands, and she talked to a lot

173

of them to see what they wanted."

"Did she bring you along?"

He laughs. "Yes. She made me wear flannel for those meetings."

I offer him the paint stick, but he just closes his eyes and leans toward me. The dingy lighting shines off his face, and I can see every freckle. There's a part of me that doesn't want to cover any of this up.

I blush, then wet the paint sticks before he realizes I'm just staring at him.

"For the record," I finally say, "I think your mom has been a pretty good mayor. But she acts like she wants everyone to get along."

"She does."

"Don't speak. You'll mess this up." I start to paint his face. "My dad said this back when she was taking political signs out of people's yards, and I never really understood what it meant until now. She doesn't want everyone to get along; she wants everyone to ignore all the problems the world, and ignore all the problems our village has, and pretend we're all best friends."

I start on the other cheek, slowly covering up those perfect freckles.

"It's like we're not allowed to fight. We're not allowed to argue or disagree. We're supposed to sit here and look like those picture-perfect small towns in movies."

A streak of red falls down his cheek, and it takes me a second to realize it's a tear.

"Brett, are you okay?"

He opens his eyes, and a few more tears fall. He shakes his head.

"I can't take the pressure anymore," he whispers.

I drop the paint stick in the sink and wrap him in a hug. Our faces press together, and I know all my work's been ruined, but he's crying harder now and I couldn't care less.

We pull apart, and I bring him down to sit on the concrete floor next to me.

"She wasn't always like this, to me. She acts like we're the First Family or something. I keep failing tests, but *all I do* is study. Nothing stays in my brain anymore, and I totally freeze up when I start to take a test, because I know how Mom will act if I even get a B."

"I don't get it, though. In math, you catch onto things way faster than me."

"And yet, I have a D in that class."

I turn to him. "How is that possible?"

"I get As on all my homework, but quizzes and tests are fifty percent of the class. It's . . . it's why I get to take all of these makeup tests. The teachers know I know the material, but I don't know how to unlock it in my brain."

"Have you talked to your mom about it? Or your dad?" I ask.

He nods. "She doesn't understand. She thinks it's some excuse I'm making. Maybe it is. I don't know."

"It doesn't sound like just an excuse," I say.

He drops his voice to a whisper. "If I could vote, I'd vote for Susan Lee."

Faintly, the sound of the band playing the fight song makes its way to the utility room. I stand and help Brett up.

"I need to wash this off," he says. "I messed it all up."

"No, it's fine. Here."

I take the slender end of the paint stick and draw wavy lines down his face. The lines mix with the faintly colored streaks where his tears fell.

"See? It's a little messy, but I think you're perfect."

I pause. "Your face is perfect, I mean." Another pause. "Your face *paint*."

"Your face is perfect, too," he says with a laugh. "Now, let's go to the game. We can't miss cheering on our school's new star cymbalist."

CHAPTER 22

"Gooooo, Barton Bulldogs! Woof, woof, woof!"

I never noticed this before, but each *woof* is accented by a cymbal crash. From the student section, I have a great view of Jenna. She's got a thick stripe of silver painted diagonally across her face, her blond hair is pulled into a side pony with pinkish-red tips, and she's rocking a bright red headband.

Over the years, I've seen her melt into dozens of friend groups, infiltrating friend groups made of drama kids, cross-country runners, the 4-H club, or the football team, but I've never seen her be more herself than when she's with the band kids.

"Hey, guys!" Ashley says while leaning over. "Love the face paint. Oh, also, Jake, I signed your petition.

Like I was telling you earlier, Columbus Pride was hands down the most fun I've *ever* had. Can't wait to have one of our own!"

"Thanks," I say. "It should be fun. Just have to see how tomorrow goes."

She assures us it'll all be fine, and then we get back to the game. The energy in the gym is unbelievable. It's so loud, the other team can barely make a basket. By halftime, we're up thirty-three to twelve.

Brett's phone rings, and I see *Mom* pop up on the screen. He groans.

"I better take this."

He gets up and leaves. The band's still playing, and I get lost in the music. Jenna's holding a cymbal up for Connor to hit alongside his snare. She's dancing in a way that makes her hair fly everywhere, which is making Connor almost cry with laughter.

It's almost like . . .

"So are you two dating?" Ashley asks as she scoots closer to me.

"No, just friends," I say.

I keep looking forward, since that's one secret I will not be spilling to *anyone*.

"Aw, that's a shame. You'd be a cute couple."

I nod. "Thanks, I guess."

"Is it weird to be friends with someone whose mom is trying to, like, crush all your dreams?"

"That's a little dramatic," I say with a laugh. "I think she'll change her mind. And even if not, I think we'll get enough council members to vote for the permit."

"I hope so," she says. "My dad's the town treasurer. He was just telling me how he's never seen this town council vote against her."

"Wait, *never*?"

"Not for the last two years, at least." She takes in my startled expression. "Oh, hey, I'm not trying to stress you out. Just trying to say how impressive it's going to be when they vote against her."

I see Brett enter the gym, and I'm a little relieved that his presence will cut off this conversation.

"Anyway, Dad may not be a voting member, but he's a big supporter. He signed the petition, too." She pats me on the back. "I'm rooting for you!"

I nod my thanks and look back to try and find Brett. But he's gone.

I know I saw him. I know he was coming up the stairs to our section. Where did he go?

The band's starting back up, and the team takes the

court. But I make my way down the stairs and through the double doors, searching for any sign of Brett.

Something tells me to look outside, so I make my way out of the doors of the school. It's dark out, and there's still a lot of people here. I walk past the groups of people toward the bench where we first got to chat not too long ago.

He sits there, hands folded in his lap, looking small. Defeated.

"Brett?" I say gently. "Can I sit down?"

He shrugs, so I take a seat next to him. His eyes don't leave his lap.

"What did your mom say?"

"I always have eyes on me." He rubs his hands together. "I *always* have eyes on me."

"What do you mean?"

He looks to me, and I see tears welling in his eyes.

"She doesn't want me hanging out with you anymore." He sighs. "One of her little . . . minions saw us at the game. I knew I couldn't hide this from her forever."

"Hiding what?" I ask. "You were hiding that you were hanging out with your neighbor?"

"My neighbor with the pride flag in his yard. My neighbor who's the only openly gay kid at school." He sighs. "My neighbor who's trying to throw Barton Springs's first pride festival."

"You're trying to throw it, too, though. You're a part of the team, remember?"

"I'm worried she knows that now, too. And if she knows that, she might know. . ." He sighs. "I can't be part of the team anymore. I'm in enough trouble."

"Okay," I say. There's a hollowness in my chest that's slowly growing. "But I like hanging out with you. It doesn't mean anything."

"I know," he says. "But I think it was starting to. For me, at least."

I blush and try to come up with a response, but I can't.

"I'm not ready, though. I can't even take a quiz without freaking out. I can't . . . figure all this out on top of everything."

He gets a text, and I see him look out into the parking lot.

"I have to go."

"Wait, maybe I can talk to her and clear things up?"

"I'm sorry, I can't. Don't hate me—"

"Brett!"

But it's too late. He disappears into the darkness.

CHAPTER 23

"He just left?" Jenna asks.

It's the first we've been able to catch up since last night's game. After our dominating lead in the first half, the other team came back with a vengeance, beating us fifty-five to fifty-two.

On the drive home, at least I didn't have to explain why I was in such a low mood.

But that was yesterday, and today is the big day, so I've tried to shake it off as much as I can. We're meeting Susan Lee for an interview before the big vote tonight. She's hopeful for a turnout, but a seed of anxiety is starting to grow inside me after hearing what Ashley said about the mayor's control over the council members.

"Was something going on between you two?" Jenna asks timidly as we walk through the park toward town hall.

As much as I want to confide in Jenna, I know I can't spill his secret, especially considering that's exactly why he had to leave.

"No, nothing," I say. It's not a lie. "But his mom was afraid people would make assumptions."

"She treats him like she treats the town," she says with a dry laugh. Her voice goes robotic. "EVERY-THING. MUST. BE. PERFECT."

I roll my eyes. "You know what sounds perfect to me? A pride festival."

"I'm with you there. But not everyone in the town feels that way." Her voice drops. "I just found a second petition this morning, but this one opposing the festival. It's already got fifty signatures."

"Of course."

"I think it'll still be okay," she says.

We make our way to town hall, where Susan Lee stands in a tan pantsuit, texting furiously. She smiles when she sees us, and gestures at a bench behind her.

"Sometimes I feel glued to my phone," she says with

a laugh. "The joys of being a Realtor. All right. I'm going to record this conversation. Are you comfortable with that?"

"I guess so?" I say.

"The focus of the story that I'm working on is the pride festival, so don't worry. I won't use a ton of quotes or do anything to put any more of the spotlight on you."

"Good," Jenna says. "Because we have enough of that. Especially Jake."

"That's what happens when your dad puts a giant pride flag in a village like this unfortunately." Susan gives us a sympathetic look. "But don't worry about all that. The *Barton Brief* is on your side, here, which is why they want me to cover this historic vote.

"First question, could you tell me why you decided to throw a pride festival in a place like Barton Springs?"

"It sounds silly," I say. "I was playing my favorite video game, *Songbird Hollow*. It's a farming simulation game where you get to live out life in this cute rural town. And I got the feeling that in the game I was accepted for who I was."

"But you didn't feel that way here in Barton Springs?"

I sigh. "Honestly, no. Even before the flag went up,

I was starting to think I'd have to leave for a bigger town someday. I thought that was the only way I could really be myself."

"You never told me that," Jenna says. "I'm so sorry."

"It was like, in every movie or book with a gay character, they were living in big towns or escaping to big cities. But then I'd play this farming game where everyone welcomed you, no matter who you were. Or I'd go to the festivals they have in town and have *so* much fun. And I was just like, why can't I stay here?"

"And you, Jenna?"

"For starters, I've always wanted to go to a pride parade. They look way cooler than anything we do here."

Susan laughs, but Jenna just shrugs. "And I guess I . . . know Jake belongs here. And I know there must be so many people like him at school and in the town. What's that corny phrase they have on the Barton Springs's website? 'The village of caring and sharing. All are welcome here'—it's about time we put action behind those words. Of everyone, the mayor should be leading this charge."

"This is all perfect. Anything else before we move on to the next topic?" Susan asks.

"Sometimes, it's hard to be proud here," I say. "I

don't even think I know what 'pride' really feels like. I think, with this festival, I was hoping I'd figure it out along the way."

We continue the interview, answering questions about the town and what we'd love to see at the village's first pride, if the vote goes through.

Eventually, she stops recording and shakes both of our hands.

"Good luck today." She gives Jenna her card. "And if all goes well, just remember that I know every business in this town. I'm not much of a party planner, but if you need sponsors or vendors, I'm here to help."

There are a lot of people against this, but it's comforting to know there are just as many who are eager to help.

Once she leaves, Jenna grabs my hand and holds it tightly.

"No one should feel like they don't belong in their own hometown," she says.

I think of Brett, who doesn't even feel like he belongs in his own family. Of all the others here who might be queer, or the others who fled the village as soon as they could just get somewhere more welcoming, somewhere safer.

I smile. "Thanks for all your help, Jenna."

"Let's do this thing."

Mom, Dad, me, and Jenna take up the front row. The meeting hasn't even started, and we're already out of seats. There's a lot of chatter behind me, but it's all muted.

My palms are sweaty, my armpits are sweaty—okay, everything is sweaty.

I do the math again. We really only need three votes, or two if we think we can sway the mayor. It'd be hard but not impossible. *Optimism, Jake.*

Jenna's dad should be a safe bet. Mr. Foley is a bit of a wild card, but Mom's been talking to him a lot lately. The other two usually side with the mayor, but the way Regina and Althea confidently strode in and smiled at us makes me think that, just maybe, they'll all be on our side.

The mayor brings everyone to order, and we're all silent. We don't know what to expect—a debate, an open forum?

"First order of business," she says, "is a request by Steven Moore. An event license to throw Barton Springs's first LGBTQ+ pride festival on town property. The council has heard more from the community on this than any issue we've ever discussed here.

"I first want to say that we take this situation very seriously, and we've taken all of your opinions to heart as we discussed and debated this matter internally."

"Why is she acting like they all don't vote separately on this?" Jenna asks.

My stomach drops when I think about how Ashley said no one's voted in opposition of the mayor in years. I let my pessimistic side take over.

"Because they don't," I say.

"We believe we've heard enough, so we won't be opening the floor to a debate. On the matter of approving the proposed festival license. Council members, a simple yea or nay will suffice."

Jenna's dad stands.

His expression looks grim, so I turn back and shoot a look to Jenna.

"He wouldn't," Jenna says, but her voice starts to tremble. "At least, I really don't think he'd—"

"Nay," he says.

Mr. Foley stands. "Nay."

The others follow suit, and the mayor nods. "Since this is a unanimous vote, I have no say." She hits a gavel.

"Permit denied."

▲ ▲ ▲

The whole car ride home, I couldn't find the words to speak to anyone. When it came to dinner, I didn't want anything. I just stayed in my room, in my bed, hiding under the covers, wanting to sleep the day away—but sleep never came.

Which is how I got here, standing on my front lawn at midnight. Staring up at the flag. The flag that once gave me hope now mocks me.

"I'll never be welcome here, will I?"

I untie the rope at the base of the flagpole.

"How can I stay? How can I keep fighting to be myself?"

The rope burns my palms as I start to lower the flag.

"If this is what the mayor wants for their perfect town? Fine."

I pull down the flag and crumple it up in my hands. I return to my room and throw the flag in my closet. I just wanted to put my head down, stick to my friends, and all it took was this stupid flag to point out what was so blatantly obvious:

I don't belong here.

CHAPTER 24

"Jake?"

I hear Jenna's voice before I see her, but that's probably because I've got the covers pulled all the way up over my head. I have no clue what time it is, but I've already decided this Sunday is for moping and *nothing* else.

She sits on the edge of my bed, but I still hide under the covers. If I keep my breaths low, maybe she'll just—

"I know you're awake."

I pull off the covers.

"How could you possibly know that?"

She laughs. "For one, you weren't snoring. I still have nightmares from all the demon noises you made from that one sleepover we had a few years ago."

"I don't snore anymore," I say. "At least, I don't think I do."

"I'm sure your parents would disagree. But anyway, I'm not here to chat about your snoring habits."

I throw the covers back over my head.

"Then what are you here for?" I ask.

"I was thinking this morning. Maybe . . . there's some other way we can do this. I know we wanted a festival in the park, but if we found some private property—maybe someone's farm? We wouldn't need a permit for that, right?"

"Sure, let's throw a backyard barbecue for ten people and call it Barton Springs's first pride."

"That's not what I'm saying, and you know it." There's an edge to her voice now, which makes anger flare up in my whole body.

"It's not about the permit," I snap. "We asked our hometown to be a *little* more accepting of people. We asked them to open their hearts a fraction of an inch, to let us have a party that they don't even have to go to. And they said—unanimously—no."

She folds her hands in her lap.

"You're right. But that doesn't mean we can't fight."

"What did your dad say?" I ask pointedly. "Why did *he* say no?"

"I didn't ask," she says firmly.

"What did he say all week when you asked him about it? You made a whole presentation, but did you ever show it to him?"

"I didn't."

"Why?" I'm trying to be firm and confident, but my voice cracks. "Why not, Jenna?"

She stands and starts to pace the room slowly. She's choosing her words, or delaying the inevitable—I don't know what's going on, but the longer she goes without answering my question, the angrier I get.

"I didn't know what he'd say," she finally says.

"You could have talked to him," I say. "Then we could have changed our strategy, or tried to convince him, or something. Did you go into that meeting thinking he'd say no?"

She shakes her head. "I thought he'd say yes, I promise I did. But I've seen him post on Facebook before with . . . questionable thoughts. He won't talk politics with me, either—I have no idea who he voted for in the last election, and I'm scared to bring it up."

"Scared of *what*?"

She balls her hands into fists. "I'm scared he's a monster, okay? He was fine with Mayor Miller snatching up those Black Lives Matter signs, but I never talked to him about it. The way he looks at your flag sometimes . . . it makes me wonder."

"If it makes you wonder, *ask*. I know it's intimidating, but you could change his mind. You know everything about every cause! You could answer his questions better than anyone, and he'd listen to you because you're his kid."

"It's not that easy," she says.

"Well, I'm glad I took down the flag last night. If I'm living next to a homophobe and an ally who's too chicken to stand up for her best friend, then I don't want it up."

"That's not fair," she says.

I shrug. "Yeah, maybe not. But you led me into thinking every council member would approve the permit, and we couldn't even get a yes from the one who lives in the *same house as you*. You said you'd ask him, and you didn't!"

"It's the mayor! She's the problem!" she says. "The only reason she knew about our plan was because you

194

told Mr. Foley, who tipped off the rest of town council. If we could have actually surprised them, we might have been able to get to a vote without the mayor interfering."

"So now it's my fault?"

"You're throwing out so much blame, I thought I might as well join the fun," she says hotly.

She reaches up to grab a lock of her hair, twisting it in her hands as she stares at my *Songbird Hollow* poster.

"Welp. I guess I shouldn't have come here, then," she says. "I thought checking up on you is what friends do, but I guess I had a whole laundry list of things I had to do first to be considered your friend, no matter how uncomfortable they make me."

"I don't want a best friend who's just fine thinking their dad might be a homophobe, if I'm honest."

"He probably isn't!" she snaps.

"*Probably* isn't good enough!"

She slams my bedroom door as she leaves, and I wait for my parents to come check on me. They don't come, so I pull the blanket back over my head.

CHAPTER 25

I haven't used my voice in about twenty-four hours, so when Mr. Foley calls my name for attendance, my voice cracks *hard* when I say, "Here."

Brett's moved back to his original seat, diagonally in front of me instead of beside me, and he's so focused on his homework, I know it's pointless to try to talk to him. A part of me really hopes he's okay, but the other part of me is causing this searing pain in my chest.

He's embarrassed to talk to me. He's embarrassed to be near me. Because of what his mom might think. Because of who I am. While Mr. Foley collects our latest assignments, Ashley taps me on the shoulder, and I turn to look at her.

"I don't know how you can stand being in the same room as Mr. Foley right now," she says, just loud enough that he can probably hear. "I think they're all cowards. If you want to fight this, you let me know."

I smile weakly. "Thanks, Ash."

"I mean it."

Throughout the rest of my classes, people mostly leave me alone. Most of them are acting just like Brett and avoiding me, but there are a few like Ashley. Kind, supportive, absolutely furious.

Even with their support, I can't face anyone. Not even Jenna. I eat lunch in the utility room for a few days, but every day I go in there gets harder. When I first came in here with Brett, all I wanted to do was lean in and plant a kiss on his cheek. And the last time, I just wanted to stare at his freckles.

Sure, my crush wasn't as intense as Jenna's, but it was something. And now it's gone, and that hurts.

The most humiliating thing, the cherry on top of this awful sundae, is that I keep finding flyers in teachers' rooms and in the halls to sign the petition. I guess Mom didn't have the heart to take them down, but I do—I promptly throw away each one I see.

▲ ▲ ▲

197

When I wake up on Friday morning, Mom reminds me that, because it's the last basketball game of the season, it's another "Barton Pride" Day, which alone makes me want to fake an illness. I can't go through the motions anymore—the Barton Bulldogs chants, the pep rallies.

I pull out a bright green shirt and put it on. In the sea of black and silver and red, I'll be a bright thorn. I don't belong in this town; they've all said as much.

They can have their chants. One day I'll have Cleveland. Or New York. Or, at least, anywhere that doesn't have a four-digit population.

I sit in the second-to-last seat on the bus. Jenna's in our usual spot behind me, and Brett's across from me with his head in a book. This is always the worst part of the day. I always try to put on a high-energy playlist so I don't get to depressed, but today's isn't cutting it.

I feel their eyes burning into me, but I know that neither of them is looking.

I lean into the window and watch my breath fog up the glass. The woods that line the final stretch to school are probably the most boring part of the trip, but now that we're in the middle of spring, the trees are bursting with bright green leaves.

Suddenly, I see a deer dart out alongside the bus. I perk up at the sight, though it's not unusual to see one out this way. It sprints ahead, and a second later, I hear our bus driver yelp.

Linda slams on the brakes, and I fly into the seat in front of me. Brett, who was hunched over, has somehow rolled onto the floor, and Jenna bursts into a fit of uncomfortable laughter.

"Everyone okay?" Linda calls back. "Damn deer came out of nowhere. Missed 'em, though!"

Brett scrambles to get up, and I offer a hand to help him back in his seat. Behind us, Jenna's still laughing, trying to control her massively disheveled hair.

Slowly, we resume our seats. We still don't talk to each other, communicating only in soft smiles. It's not much . . . but it's not nothing.

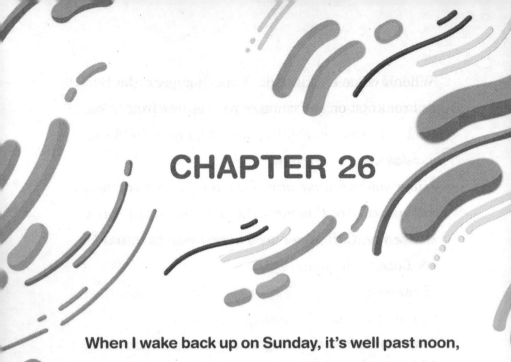

CHAPTER 26

When I wake back up on Sunday, it's well past noon, and I find it odd my parents still haven't checked up on me. After this awful week, I feel like I got hit by a dump truck, and there's a part of me that's begging for some sort of attention. Or at least confirmation that everything *is* the worst, and it's okay that I feel this way.

I check every room. I check the front porch. They're not around, and a car is missing from the garage.

On the porch, I look up to the flagpole, which has been empty for a week. It reminds me that Jenna wanted to keep fighting, and Brett wanted to give up. What did I want? What *do* I want?

I still don't really know.

When I come back inside, I notice a bag of McDonald's breakfast on the counter with a note from Mom.

Jake,

Hope you're feeling okay. Dad and I had something to take care of this morning, but we didn't want to wake you. Call if you need us, we'll be back soon.

Love,

Mom

I figure there's no use pouting and sulking to an empty room, so I eat breakfast, shower, and put on one of my many Barton Bulldogs shirts.

This is temporary, I remind myself. I've read plenty of books about leaving home after high school, finding your own family, and making it on your own. I could do that.

I try to ignore the fact that I . . . don't want to.

But I could.

I return to my bedroom to play some *Songbird Hollow* and wait for my parents to come back. I keep thinking about what happened on the bus on Friday, and how I could have so easily gone back to sit with Jenna. But I know she's okay. She's been with Connor more often lately, and she's surrounded by a whole new group of band friends.

While I leave the game on to wait for the perfect time to harvest my sweet potatoes—it's now winter in my game—I jump onto the *Songbird* forums. I realize I haven't updated anyone on what happened last week.

I see I have a ton of replies on my thread, but I check my direct messages first, to see if Robert, the guy who threw his town's first pride, too, responded to our last exchange. He did, and it looks urgent.

Jake—don't go into your thread. I got one of the moderators to lock the forums down, but it's going to take a while to get everyone blocked.

My heart drops into my stomach. This little section of the internet, just like Songbird Hollow itself, was my safe space. It was the sheltered little world where me and a bunch of other nerds shared tips on growing virtual fruits and vegetables.

I click into the forum and immediately flinch.

It's like when a bunch of seniors spray-painted all over the high school for last year's senior prank. What was once pristine and innocent is now drowning in homophobia and abuse.

On the one hand, I don't want to read the words.

But a part of me—the darker one, the side of me who took down the flag—wants to see this. Wants to know exactly who I'm up against in the world.

When Dad told Granny I was gay, she didn't say anything good or bad. What she said was "I don't want him to have such a hard life." It's also what some of the teachers have told my mom.

But too often, it's like I'm the only one fighting to make this life easy for myself. I can have a hard life—does anyone have an *easy* life?—but I wonder if the people who say that know how much power they have to take on the burden.

They can make my life easier. They're just choosing not to.

I can't get all the hateful messages I saw out of my head. It's like every time I blink, a new awful word is written on my eyelids. I look down and fold my hands in my lap, and that's when I hear the familiar sound of Mom's car pulling into the driveway. I look to the window and see Mom and Dad get out, and I briefly consider running down the stairs and jumping into their arms for comfort like I'd do when I was a kid.

But I don't. A tear slips down my cheek, which feels extra silly considering the cutesy winter music from *Songbird Hollow* is still playing on repeat. I close out of the game and open the system data menu, staring at the *Delete Save Data* option.

I'm going to do it. Homophobes truly ruin everything.

"Hey, Jake," Dad says, opening my door. "Did you get our— Whoa, buddy, what's wrong?"

I wipe away a tear. He takes the controller away from me and wraps me in a tight hug, and more tears fall. I don't know how to explain this to him, so I just shake him off me, go to my laptop, and open the thread.

"Look." It's the only word I can get out without fully losing it.

He takes a minute to read through the thread, though I see that a few comments have already been removed by the forum's moderator.

"Wow," Dad finally says. "People are . . . *really* awful, aren't they?"

"It's just . . . *Songbird Hollow* was my safe space, you know?"

He nods. "It still can be, right? That website has nothing to do with—" He gestures toward the screen and sees the *Delete Save Data* option. "Oh, Jake, don't delete it. This is still your space. With—what's his name? Patrick? And the golden oysters."

"Peter," I say with a laugh. "And golden seashells. But you were really close."

Dad wipes a tear from my cheek and takes a seat next to me on the bed.

"I'm not sure what to say," he finally says, "but I want you to remember that you have a lot of support. Mom says she keeps seeing little pride flags and pins all over the school now. I know *Songbird Hollow* means a lot to you, and you'll always have that—even if it takes a while to forget the awful things on that website."

He squeezes my shoulder and gives me a supportive smile.

"But I think you have Barton Springs, too."

CHAPTER 27

Around lunchtime, Mom knocks on my door and says we're going for a ride. I hesitate briefly, but when she mentions Taco Bell is involved, I'm out the door in a flash. Once we've secured the goods—a whole bag of bean burritos—my suspicion starts to set in, and I realize I have no idea where we're going.

"Can you at least tell me where you've been?" I ask between bites of my burrito.

Dad looks to my mom in the driver's seat. She nods slightly.

"We went to an open house," he finally says.

I almost spit a dangerously large amount of beans out on my lap. We're looking for a new house? Just because Barton Springs didn't want to throw a festival in their park? What happened to the whole "I think you have Barton Springs, too" thing?

Outside my window, the fields morph into the lot for Barton Elementary School, where I stayed until fifth grade, then the middle school. Two places I've spent literal years of my life. Sure, I might have to leave Barton Springs after I graduate, but I didn't think we'd be leaving *now*.

"We're *moving*?" I say. I'm furious. "Just like that?"

As much as I'd love to live in a place that's more accepting, after Dad's pick-me-up convo, so much of me wants to stay.

Maybe I'm not ready to give up.

The thought passes quickly, before Dad flips back in his seat.

"Oh god, no, we're not moving Jake," he says quickly. "I'm sorry, I now totally get how that sounded."

"Why else would you be going to an open house?" I ask.

Without taking her eyes off the road, Mom reaches into the purse next to Dad and pulls out a brochure. She passes it my way.

"We needed to have a chat," she says, "with her."

The house on sale looks nice, but I know that's not

the point. The headshot in the corner tells me everything I need to know: property listed by Susan Lee of
Susan Lee Realty and Auctioneering.

Eventually, we make it to the park, and we take the
same seats we did when we first started our scheming,
not too long ago.

"This morning, we picked up the *Barton Brief,* and
we were shocked to find a picture of you and Jenna
on page three."

"Oh," I say. "The interview went out? I assumed
Susan scrapped it when the vote went the other way."

Dad hands the paper over to me, and I unfold it.
This page doesn't look like the others. It doesn't look
like Susan's first article—in fact, it barely looks like
an article at all.

At the bottom, the words "Susan Lee for Mayor" are
written in huge letters.

"This looks like an ad," I finally say.

"It *is* an ad. You can read it all if you want, but she
took a lot of your interview. You and Jenna were so
excited, so hopeful."

"But so was Susan, I thought?"

"We weren't so sure," Mom says. "So we talked to
her. First of all, to remind her that using minors in

political ads without parental permission is not legal."

"We were trying to get a real read on her," Dad says. "She wants to use this pride festival as a jumping-off point for her campaign."

"Looks like she already did," I reply.

A voice behind me says, "Maybe I can take over?"

It's Susan Lee.

"Thanks for giving me a chance to explain myself," she says to my parents. "Is Jenna not here?"

"She's not," I say.

"Well, hopefully you can pass along my apology." She takes a deep breath. It hisses through her teeth. "You two were the perfect spokespeople for this. Jake, you're an openly gay teen with supportive parents—I mean, we've all seen the flag. Jenna, she was a straight ally who wanted to support her friend, no matter what."

I look down, and I feel bad for going off on Jenna.

"Not to mention, your mom is so connected at the school and your dad comes from one of the oldest families in this town. I knew you all could make real change, and *that* is what I've been trying to do with my campaign."

"Then tell us," I say. "Why keep me in the dark if you really thought the town council would smack it down?"

"I guess I had some hope—personally, I wanted them to look into your hopeful faces and finally break free of the mayor's grasp. But when they each said no, it showed half the town exactly who was in control. It's not the people. It's not the town council. It's *her*."

"Jake," Mom says tenderly. "We saw that you took down the flag."

I nod.

"I said it from the beginning—if you want it down, we'll keep it down. But I want you to know people are really upset about this ruling."

Susan cuts in. "For the last four years, we've had a June festival. One was paid for by the town for the Founders Day anniversary. One year we had *two* antique car shows in June. And before that, we hosted the county's Strawberry Festival two years in a row."

I laugh. "Jenna should have asked you for help putting together that binder. You know everything about Barton."

"There's room for this festival, is what I'm saying."

"Since last night, your petition has been spread around the county—getting more than eight hundred signatures." Dad clears his throat. "Uncle Jeremy and

Aunt Bonnie teamed up to tag everyone they knew on Facebook."

"Wow," I say. "What a duo."

"I think we have a lot more conversations to have as a family. But the point is that . . . if you're still interested. We can do it. We can try."

Susan stands and puts a supportive palm on my shoulder.

"I said it before, and I meant it—if you need help funding it, I can get you the business sponsors. You just need a venue that isn't scared of the mayor and isn't owned by the town. Which will be tricky."

We head home, but I don't talk much. I'm not sure if there's anything else to say—again, it's up to me. Do I want to try and patch things up with Jenna? Do I want to try this whole thing over again?

Coming the back way through the town, I watch the corn growing outside the car window, begging for an answer to pop up from the ground and tell me what to do.

We're at the bus stop where Ashley Ortega usually gets off, sometimes alone or with a gaggle of her 4-H club friends. I think of the conversations she's had with me over the last few months, and I'm reminded that Jenna and I, and maybe Brett, really aren't the only ones who wanted to see Barton Pride.

At the front of her lawn is a lawn sign with a pride flag on it.

I take it as a sign. So, I send two texts: one to Jenna, and one to Brett. They both say the same thing:

Can we talk? My front porch, ten minutes?

"Well, how about that?" Dad says, pointing to Ashley's pride sign, and I can hear the smile in his voice. "I think this town might be changing after all."

CHAPTER 28

When we get back to the house, my parents go inside, but I take a seat on one of the rocking chairs on the porch. Five, ten minutes pass. I curl my legs up on the chair and start rocking.

My texts both say *Read*, but I don't see any movement from either house.

Mom peeks out of the door. "Still nothing?"

I shrug. "Not yet."

"You know you can wait inside, right?"

"Yeah, but I want them to see me here waiting for them."

"Thought that might be the case," she says. She tosses me a Barton Bulldogs hoodie. "The wind's really picking up. Don't catch a cold."

The sky dims, and I smell the rain before it even comes. I listen hard for the coming raindrops, but instead, I hear a screen door squeak open.

I gasp, turning behind me to see a blur tiptoeing out of the front door of Jenna's house. It's heading my way in long strides, and as she gets closer, it's obvious to see it's Jenna. She makes it to the porch and wipes moisture from her hair.

"You're still here," she says. There's a warmth in her voice, which I appreciate, because I didn't really want to fight.

"Figured I'd stay here until you came out."

She takes the other rocking chair. "And if I didn't?"

"I wasn't letting myself panic about that just yet." I fold my hands in my lap and sigh. "Okay, I was panicking a bit."

"So what's up? What's the big news?"

"Did you see the paper today?"

"Oh, yeah," she says with a laugh, "I think I'm grounded? Dad sent me to my room because apparently a councilperson's daughter doing ad campaigns against the mayor isn't a good look?"

"Did you explain?"

She shrugs. "I mean, she could have been like, 'This

214

interview is paid for by the Anyone-but-Miller-for Mayor Committee' and I would have still been like, okay, sign me up."

I roll my eyes. "Jenna, be serious."

"Well, truthfully? He got mad at me for something I didn't do, so I leaned in and asked him if he felt betrayed? If he felt abandoned by the one person who should always be on his side?"

"So you laid on the guilt for his vote, is what you're saying."

"Exactly," she says, rocking her chair back as far as it'll go. "It was amazing. We got to a point where I realized I was already in trouble for talking back, so I might as well straight up ask him why he was acting like a homophobe."

"Oh god, you didn't?"

The rain comes, at first in soft patters, then quickly escalating into downpour status. The tin roof pops above me a million times a minute. We have to raise our voices to talk over the noise.

"I did. We had a long talk. We were so mad at the beginning, but he finally let down the walls on how Mayor Miller controls them. Did you know she can ban them from local office at any point? When she took over four years ago, there were eight council members. Now there are four. I'll let you draw your own conclusions."

"What a . . . wild abuse of power," I say.

"I asked why he still stays if he's literally scared of her. Want to know what he said? He still thinks that she has the best vision for the village." She sighs. "You know, I wanted to apologize about something else."

"Yeah?" I ask.

"I don't think I could have changed his mind about the vote, but I didn't even try. I didn't want to make him mad. I didn't want to call him out and have him be defensive. I thought I could just be a big enough ally for the two of us." Her eyes meet mine. "But if I was actually an ally, I would have confronted him from the start. So, I guess I was a bad ally, and a bad friend for a bit. I'm sorry."

"You were never a bad friend," I say, "but thanks."

"Oh, speaking of apologies! Dad says he's sorry he wasn't more supportive of the flag, and he said we can get a sign for our yard, too, if I wanted."

I raise my voice to shout over the rain.

"Until the mayor steals them all."

"Until my mom does *what*?" Brett shouts back. Through all the noise, I didn't hear him coming up the dark driveway.

Jenna brushes something off her shoulder dismissively. "Does your mom know you're here, hanging out with two honorary team members of mayoral candidate Susan Lee?"

Brett laughs. "No, honestly, she'd kill me. What did you guys do?"

"We thought we were being interviewed for another fluff piece for the paper, not accidentally launching Susan's mayoral campaign." I sigh. "But that's actually what I want to talk to you about.

"Susan apologized for taking advantage of us, and she said she really did hope the pressure from the town would influence the mayor. But she did say that, if we can get over the sting of this, we could still do this."

"You mean . . . the whole pride festival?" Brett asks.

"Yeah. Just not in the park. We'd have to find private property big enough to host something like this."

"I can think of plenty of farms, I guess," Jenna says. "But they don't have public bathrooms or a ton of electricity."

"I can't think of anywhere, either. But maybe we can do some research and figure it out? Brett, would you want to help us?"

He looks to us both and smiles. "I want to help. I'm not ready to be out—I want you both to know that. I don't know if it's safe for me." He pauses, then turns to Jenna. "Oh, Jenna, I'm bi. I guess I should have started with that."

"Noted," she says. "I'm honored you feel comfortable telling me, and your secret is totally safe with me."

"Can you still hang out with us, though?" I ask. "I miss y—I mean, I miss seeing you around."

Jenna nods toward Brett, so only I can see. She give a kissy face and a wink, and I roll my eyes.

"Okay, I'm still half-grounded, so I need to get back," Jenna says with a laugh. "I'm going to make an addendum to the petition and try to get more support."

"And I guess we'll brainstorm other places to host an event like this," I say. "Before you go, Jenna, I'm really sorry for snapping at you."

"Apology accepted," she says. "I'm sorry to both of you. Jake, I was just as snippy with you, when really we should have been directing all of our anger at the problem. Brett, sorry if I pressured you too much to be a part of this. I didn't mean to make you uncomfortable."

She pulls us into a group hug before sprinting back to her house, screaming as the rain soaks her through.

"Hey, Brett, want to take her spot?"

Brett takes the other rocking chair, and he's just inches from me. I'm still not the expert on crushes, really, but I'm excited to be near him. Seeing him smile for the first time in a week has been incredible.

"Since we're all apologizing, I'm sorry for walking out on you at the basketball game." He sighs. "I don't know why I was so scared. One of Mom's friends saw us together in matching face paint and assumed something about me."

"Do you think your mom knows?"

He shrugs. "I bet I'll come out to her someday and she'll be like, 'I knew all along!' but really . . . no. She didn't want others to assume that I was a part of the pride festival plan, and thus, against her. But damn, this week sucked. I couldn't talk to you all week because I knew I'd hurt you. Oh, and I started seeing a therapist."

"Therapy? For what?"

"I think I have to do summer school. My grades aren't improving, and I can't stop panicking anytime a test is in front of me." He breathes slowly. "Mom and Dad finally realized we should talk to someone, and the therapist made them stay in the room so we could talk about the pressure they're putting on me. I'm starting solo sessions soon, too, for general anxiety."

"I'm sorry you have to do that," I say. "I don't know much about anxiety, but I've read books with characters who have it. Might be helpful? I got a lot of queer books from the library when I was starting to figure out my sexuality, and it really helped me understand myself more."

He reaches over and places his hand over mine. "Thanks. Once I catch up on grades and homework, I'll take you up on that."

"I should get back soon. Mom's going to think I'm a runaway or something."

"Will you help us with the pride festival? I know you have a lot going on, but I want you there. I want your help. We can keep it a secret from your mom and everything.

"I don't want it to be a secret," he says. He opens his umbrella and starts to walk out into the rain. "I'll help, but only if you'll let me get my mom on board with it."

"What? How?"

"I have an idea! But you're going to have to let me pray on it."

I have no idea what that means, but I let him go. He walks slowly down the driveway, and I see him close his umbrella and stare into the pouring rain.

"Come over here!" he shouts. "Have you ever just gotten absolutely drenched for no reason?"

I step under the curtain of water and walk out to him. My body urges me to run, but instead, I take slow steps. I look up and let the rain run all the way from my head to my toes.

Without thinking much, I reach out to Brett, and I pull him in for a hug. He fits nicely inside my embrace, and for one brief second, he leans his head into mine.

"See you at school, yeah?"

I'm glad it's too dark to see the blush across my face. "Yeah. Night, Brett."

"Good night, Jake." He turns to go, then flips back to call out one more time: "You give really good hugs! Just . . . thought you should know."

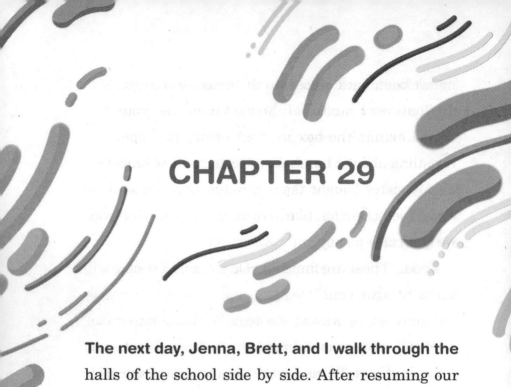

CHAPTER 29

The next day, Jenna, Brett, and I walk through the halls of the school side by side. After resuming our normal seating arrangement on the bus, I feel unstoppable. Town hall showed us just how easily "stopped" we are, but with more than a thousand signatures for our petition, and coverage and other local papers, we're seeing support come out from all over the place.

When I get to my locker, I see Ashley waiting for me. She's holding a box in front of her, and when I approach, she not-so-secretly hides it behind her back.

"Oh, wow, the whole pride gang's here," she says with a laugh. "My sister sent that petition to all her old high school friends. She said she'd come back for a visit if we end up throwing our own pride, and she hasn't been back since winter break, so I'm going to do whatever I can to help you get it off the ground."

She brings the box in front of her and opens it, revealing about a hundred silicone rainbow bracelets.

"My sister bought these in bulk, and she said we should sell them for, like, five dollars a pop. That way, we can raise money *and* awareness."

I nod. "These are fantastic. Do you think people will actually buy them?"

"Okay, so—I was at Robbie's birthday party this weekend, and I was talking to him, Rissa, Jayme, and a couple others. Turns out they *really* wanted the pride festival to happen."

I lean back, a little surprised that Rissa and Jayme— our star volleyball players—and Robbie—our star basketball player—all casually supported our cause.

"I figured we could use them as influencers, since everyone in our little school copies them for literally everything. So, I gave them all a bracelet, and if it's okay with you, they'll post to their Instagram about the fundraiser."

I look in my wallet and find a twenty-dollar bill, totally unspent from my last allowance.

"I'm in," I say, trading in the twenty for four bracelets.

"We're going to need all the money we can get."

I hand out all the bracelets, then give the extra to Jenna, to pass along to Connor.

"I've got a venue in mind," Brett says, and we all turn to him. "But I have to talk to someone first. It would be free, but they make everyone put down a deposit, in case anything gets broken."

Jenna leaves to go meet Connor before first period and give him his bracelet, so Ashley, Brett, and I go into the classroom.

"All right, they're all posting to Instagram now. Now everyone will know to come find me if they want to be one of the cool kids," she says with a laugh.

Mr. Foley looks up, with a hint of concern on his face.

"Fundraisers aren't allowed, unless they're part of an official school activity," he says. "Ashley, come here."

It feels like all the blood leaves my face when she takes her box up to Mr. Foley's desk, knowing our fundraiser could be over before it even started.

He reaches into his wallet and pulls out a bill that's *much* larger than a five. Ashley hands him a bracelet, a little stunned, before he says, "You're going to want to put this in a backpack, or something—the box is really obvious. Stay clear of Ms. Hardin and Mr. Harris, they'd absolutely snitch. I'll give a heads-up to some of the teachers. As long as the principal doesn't catch you, you should be okay. Got it?"

Ashley nods. "Thanks, Mr. Foley."

He looks to me and gives me a wink. I still kind of hate him for going along with the mayor, but after what Jenna said about the control Mayor Miller has on her town council . . . maybe he does support us. I just wish he'd have shown his support when it actually counted, but I guess this counts, too.

After the morning announcements, Mr. Foley hands out this week's quiz. I hear Brett take a deep breath next to me.

"You gonna be okay?" I ask.

"Not sure. My therapist taught me some breathing techniques, though. And Mom hasn't been breathing down my neck quite as much lately. *And* I know this like the back of my hand."

"You're going to nail this," I say.

He nods. "Thanks, Jake."

We move from class to class. I spot Rissa in the halls, and she gives me a smile and shows off the bracelet on her wrist. At lunch, it seems every other person has one on.

When I go to throw away my trash, I spot my mom.

"Seems like there's an unsolicited fundraiser going on in here," she says conspiratorially.

"Officially, I have no idea what you're talking about."

She laughs and pulls up her sleeve to reveal a bracelet. "Officially, neither do I."

In science, we spend the whole period putting the finishing touches on our projects. Ms. Nugent calls me up to her desk.

"Hi, Jake," she says. "I just wanted to know if you have any concerns going into the presentation."

I shake my head. "I've got it all pretty much done. I suck at public speaking, but all the words are there."

I hand over the sheet of paper, and Ms. Nugent gives it a quick look. "I think you'll do fine, but you know what I'd suggest? Why don't you write down the main point for each paragraph on a note card, and try giving this presentation without reading your paper?"

"No way," I say quickly, then cover my mouth. "Sorry, don't tell Mom I said that. What I mean is—"

"Let me explain. I heard you give your presentation

here, and I heard you give one at the town hall meeting, and I think you need to stop reading from a piece of paper and speaking from the heart."

"From the heart? About carbon dating?"

She laughs. "Yes. You know the material. You know what you need to say. Use those nerves to your advantage, and just talk."

"Either way, I won't be as good as Brett."

"You don't have to be. We're all good at different things. He's probably good at public speaking because he's had a lot of practice since his mother is a politician. I think you'll be just as good if you look up from the paper, make eye contact with people, and give in to this process."

I head toward the band room at the end of the day to find Jenna. The drumline's going out for pizza after practice, so that's worth spending an extra hour at school, in my opinion.

As I walk into the band room, Jenna and the other cymbal player are working on tricks—she crashes them up in the air and spins them down. They work on a drill where the snares keep a beat, and Jenna practices crashing and muting her cymbals to the beat.

It's wild there's so much you can do with one instrument, and it's also so cool how much music you can make with just a handful of drums and cymbals.

She looks fully in her element, so much so that she hasn't spotted me, hanging in the back of the room sitting in a plastic chair. At the end of the practice session, they all "high-five" with their instruments.

Connor and Jenna have a whole routine, and the others all tap their drumsticks and mallet. When Zack taps Jenna's cymbal with a mallet, I see his bracelet.

"Jake!" Jenna says. "How'd I do?"

"You made loud noises!"

"Perfect—goal achieved!"

After they all put away their instruments, we walk down the street to the town's only pizza place. I hang back, watching Jenna interact with her new friends.

She steal's Connor's drumsticks and does an obnoxious baton show with them, tossing them into the air with the poise of a ballerina. The others laugh—now who said all those dance lessons would never pay off?

"Hey, man." Connor falls back and puts his arm on my shoulder. "You ever gonna put that flag back up?

We pass it on our bus, too, and I miss seeing it around."

"Who's on your bus?"

He shrugs. "Hmm. Pretty much anyone who lives out past Old Barton Springs Road, so Adam, Caleb, Kevin, and, of course, Queen Rissa."

We stay a few paces behind Jenna, who's still one hundred percent class-clowning it up for her new friends. I have to physically stop myself from cringing.

"Did any of them say anything about the flag when Dad put it up? Like, was it a big deal?"

"It was a big deal for, like, a day." Connor furrows his eyebrows. "I don't think anyone was upset, if that's what you're asking. Oh, Carl said it was weird, but Rissa was like, 'You're weird,' and that pretty much put an end to it."

I laugh so hard I have to stop walking. "That's it? That's really it? Just a 'You're weird' comeback was all it took?"

He shrugs. "I never quite understood the true power of the popular people."

We get to the pizza place, and I see the only employee's eyes widen at the sight of a hyped-up teen drumline pour into the restaurant.

"Looks like you're getting close with everyone," I say. "Even Zack."

"I mean, he's real cute." Her eyes linger for a couple seconds. "But totally not my type. I can't believe I was so obsessed with him without even knowing him. But we've hung out a few times since I joined the drumline. He's been teaching me how to march so I'll be ready for marching band next year."

"And Connor?"

She blushes. "Now that boy is my type."

"Jenna Thomas, marching band geek. I honestly don't think I ever saw that coming."

She laughs. "My dad always says it's good to try everything out. That's why he put me in dance class, T-ball, soccer, child improv classes—"

"Hold up. I knew about all the others," I say, remembering that awful year we were on the T-ball team together, "but I've *never* heard you talk about 'child improv classes.'"

"Yeah, at the community center," she says, her face beaming red. "It's the most embarrassing thing I've ever done. I promised I would never tell a soul."

"Please tell me there's video evidence," I say, and she nods.

"Oh, there is, but you'll never see it." She pauses to think. "Wait, actually, how about this? That cursed DVD will be my graduation gift to you, but only if we stay best friends until then."

"Oh, this friendship is never going away." I pause. "Not with that kind of incentive."

CHAPTER 30

According to Ashley's last update, we've fully run out of bracelets, and we're raking in the dough. Her sister is shipping another box her way, but we still don't have a venue, and I'm starting to get stressed.

Dad said we could use our yard in a pinch, but that just seems sad. We want something big, somewhere with a lot of space. We're not throwing a birthday party; we're throwing a huge celebration for the town—even if the town doesn't want to officially be a part of it.

"Jenna's at the dentist, right?" Brett asks, following me onto the bus. "Can we sit together?"

"Sure," I say with a smile.

I scootch into my seat, and he takes the spot next to me. My brain keeps reminding me that his hands are *right there*, and if I reached for one, and he let me, we could hold hands and no one would see us.

"You're sweating," he says.

I laugh. "Maybe it'll help that I'm breathing in anti-perspirant right now."

"Not again," he says as he sniffs himself. "I did what Linda said, just a spray here, here, and—"

"I'm joking. You smell good, and I can breathe."

"Whew," he says. "All right, I have something to ask you. And it's a little . . . weird."

"Sure?" I say, anticipation pounding in my chest.

"Would you come to church with me tonight? I've been talking with my pastor for a while about . . . a lot of things. And she says she can help with the pride festival."

"I haven't been to church in years," I say. "And I remember exactly when it was. Our pastor had this whole sermon trying to explain why it was okay for us to treat immigrants like monsters here in the US. He'd gotten a lot of pushback for his views on Face-book or something. Something he posted went viral, and everyone kept talking about how nothing he was saying matched the teachings of Jesus. And we just kind of stopped going."

"I'm sorry," he says. "Not all churches are like that, you know."

"I know, but it's the only church Dad's family had ever gone to. I think Mom and Dad talked about joining another, but eventually realized they didn't want to. I just liked having Sunday mornings free to play my video games."

He nods. "Well, anyway. I'm not asking you to join a church or anything. But I do want you to talk to our pastor, and Mom doesn't usually come to Wednesday-evening services."

"Okay, I'm in."

When I get back home, I rush through my homework and tell Mom I have plans with Brett.

"What plans?" she says.

"I . . . don't want to tell you."

"Well, that isn't suspicious or anything."

"Okay, fine. He wants me to go to church with him. His pastor wants to help out with the pride festival somehow."

"Oh, okay. That's good timing anyway. Let's do an early dinner because I'm going over to talk to Susan Lee about finding corporate donors and booking vendors."

She finally agrees to let me go, knowing that's too elaborate of a lie for me to come up with—not that I have a habit of lying to them on issues like this.

I dress up for church in khakis and a crisp white polo. To be honest, I don't really remember how to dress for church, so I've decided to cosplay as Brett.

Brett tells me he's outside. He's on his bike.

"Do you have a bike?"

"Uhhh, I think it has a flat tire," I say, not explaining I haven't ridden a bike in literal years.

"Thought that might be the case." He tosses me a helmet. "Hop on the back."

Unsteadily, I mount the back of his bike.

"Where do I put my hands?"

He laughs. "My shoulders? My waist? Whatever's comfortable."

I keep my hands on his shoulders the whole time, and the ride's so enjoyable I think about having Dad fill up the tires in my bike again.

Church service starts, and I go through the motions. I never had much of a connection to the church, having only gone out of obligation for years and years. Even as a kid, I didn't get it. At least this pastor seems nice.

I sing the hymns next to Brett.

I close my eyes as Brett prays.

I don't know what it's like for him, but he seems happy here. And part of that must be Pastor Nicole. After the congregation starts to leave, she waves me and Brett into her office. She shakes my hand and welcomes me warmly to the church.

"Brett, my dear, how did the math exam go?"

I turn, realizing I didn't even ask.

"We don't get grades back until Monday, but it went well, I think. I only froze up a couple times, and I was able to finish the whole quiz, so that's progress."

"Congrats, Brett!"

He leans to me. "Pastor Nicole is the one who put us in touch with that therapist. It's been a huge help."

"All right, so I'm excited to talk to you all about this potential pride festival. But this time, I can't do it alone. Brett, anything you've said to me in confidence is still purely in confidence, okay? But I can't do all of this behind your mom's back."

He shrugs. "I guess that makes sense."

There's a firm knock on the door.

"That's her," she says in a whisper. "Let's work through this, okay?"

236

The door opens, and Brett's mom steps into the small space. She takes off her light jacket and pulls back when she sees me, before quickly recovering with a smile.

She takes a seat, and we all stare in awkward silence before Nicole's calming voice lowers all of our heart rates.

"Look, we can't get through this without a lot of honesty," Pastor Nicole says. "I'll start. I think this town needs a place where LGBTQ+ townspeople of all ages can feel safe. There are many forms this can take, and we're already making progress on one of them—the trustees here just approved the creation of an LGBTQ+ support club that'll meet biweekly here."

"Okay," Mayor Miller says. "That's good for them. They need a space like this."

"I also agree with Jake and your son—I think these people need a celebration. I have a lot of resources that I give to teachers and anyone who works with LGBTQ+ youth that I'll email to you right now. Essentially, you'll learn that there are a lot of queer people out there. And when they don't receive the support they need, at best? They leave and find a welcoming environment, and they still deal with this trauma their whole lives. *At best.*"

"How is this my responsibility? When I signed up for this, I wanted to clean up the town, improve the schools, all things that a mayor needs to do." She scrunches her eyebrows. "I've also made this town a more peaceful place."

"Taking people's signs and not letting people speak their mind isn't making the town a more peaceful place," I say.

"He's right," Brett chimes in. "People are coming to you with a problem, and your only response is to bury it."

"Susan Lee has really gotten into their heads," Mayor Miller says, but the pastor just shakes her head.

"Look," the pastor says, "maybe to you and Susan this is all politics. I don't care. What I care about is celebrating the diversity in our community and making *everyone* feel safe. I firmly believe that should be the mayor's job, too. This Sunday, I'm going to propose allowing Mr. Moore to rent the church grounds for the festival.

"Unlike at the town council meetings, every church member will have a voice, and we'll come to a decision together. It won't be a vote. I'm not breaking any ties. I will facilitate the conversation, but I won't even introduce the suggestion."

"Who will?" Mayor Miller asks.

"I will," Brett says, nodding confidently at the pastor.

We ride home at night, choosing to take the bike over Mayor Miller's offer to drive us. Brett takes a hard right into a dark country road with no lights. The houses are all set back, and we're flanked by fields of corn and soy.

"Do you think it'll work?" I ask.

He laughs. "No clue. But I think people will actually listen this time. Maybe Mom can get some pointers on how to run town hall meetings from this."

"It was brave of you to stand up to your mom like that."

"Thanks, Jake. She said we're going to have a long talk tonight. I don't know what to expect from her, but I know what I'm going to say. I'm going to tell her everything, about how her breathing down my neck is making my anxiety so much worse. How much she's changed since taking office."

"You ready for that?"

"I think I am. She's going to regret giving me all those lessons for our science project—I'm about to give *her* one hell of a presentation."

We slowly walk down the street, our shoulders bouncing lightly off each other. The only sound I hear is the clicking of Brett's bike chain as he pushes it alongside him. I look up, and thousands of stars greet me. It's a new moon and a crystal-clear night. I try to spot constellations, planets, or anything else out here, but I realize that for all the science tests I've aced, I still don't know much about space.

When Brett reaches out to me, lacing his soft fingers through mine, I suck in a breath. He squeezes my hand lightly, and I squeeze back tightly.

"I've wanted to do that for a while," he says. "Your hand's so warm."

"I could do this all night," I say, knowing that our parents will freak out if we're not back in the next few minutes.

"One day, we will."

"Yeah," I reply. "One day."

CHAPTER 31

Even though he's been our neighbor since I can remember, I still don't know much about Jenna's dad. He keeps to himself, mostly; he's a lawyer for a firm in Akron, but he almost always works remotely from his home office. He doesn't talk to me much, and whenever my parents hang out with him, I'm usually off playing video games with Jenna.

But one thing I *do* know? He is a grill master.

Jenna had the idea to throw this spontaneous midday cookout between our two families on Sunday, while we wait for news from Brett about his church's vote. She invited Ashley and Connor, whose parents dropped them off about a half hour ago.

I look back at our texts from the morning, and I wish

I could be there with him to see how the vote turns out. But it's not our decision. It's not our congregation. And while they always welcome visitors, this is something they need to do on their own.

So, we nervously eat hot dogs and listen to Dad's early 2000s pop punk playlist. Jenna keeps casually strolling by his phone, waiting for a moment to switch it to a better playlist, but until then, we bob our heads noncommittally to the angsty music.

My parents start unloading the side dishes onto the large picnic table out back, while I go to retrieve the last of the burgers and hot dogs from Jenna's dad.

"Hey, buddy," he says. "It'll be another minute. Just going to melt the cheese on these burgers."

"Sounds good," I say.

"You'll be happy to know we got ourselves the same pride sign that your friend Ashley got. I'd put up a flagpole of our own if we could afford it," he says with a kind chuckle, "but at least it's something."

I don't reply right away, so he continues. "Jake, I— How do I say this? I'm sure Jenna's told you all my excuses, but I wanted to tell you I'm real sorry for what I put you through back at that vote. Mr. Foley and I got to talking, and we both realized how much we were hurting you and Jenna by not wanting to disagree with Angela—er, Mayor Miller."

"It's not just me and Jenna, you know? It's like I said at the meeting: it's a message to every queer kid saying they're not wanted here. I know that wasn't your intention, but that's definitely how some people could take it."

He starts to pile burgers on my plate. "I appreciate you telling me that. We've had some closed-door meetings with her about it, and I think we'll have many more. It's pretty clear that if she wants to win reelection, she needs to stop trying to control the whole town. Even Althea spoke up about it, and I've never seen her advocate for anything other than the status quo." He sighs. "Anyway, we're going to do the work to make this town as welcoming as it should be. I'm even going to try and get your dad to run for town council someday."

I smile. "Now *that* sounds like a good idea."

Back at the picnic table, I take large spoonfuls of macaroni salad and potato salad (and pretty much any other mayonnaise-based "salad") and pass the bowls along to everyone else.

"The debate should be happening now," Mom says.

"Conversation," I correct. "Pastor Nicole was very clear that it was nothing like what she witnessed at town hall."

I catch Jenna shooting her dad a pointed look.

"Just don't get your hopes up too much," I say. "I don't know if I can handle that kind of disappointment again."

Dad puts his hand on my shoulder. "I know you can. And that's why I'm choosing blind optimism."

"Make sure you save some for Brett and the Millers, just in case," Mom says as I reach for another scoop of potato salad.

"You made a gallon of each," Dad jokes lightly.

"I've seen our family go through more *and* faster."

"Excuse me, Mrs. Moore?" Ashley asks. "So let's say they say it's okay. What do we do next? We don't have much time left to plan."

"The venue's the hardest part," Mom says. "At least, that's what Susan tells me. As soon as we get a date and a location, Susan says she will sign up a few corporate sponsors, and we can use that money to book a few local bands."

"She isn't going to turn it into some campaign event, right?" Jenna asks.

Mom nods. "She's not playing the politics card this

time. All she wanted to do was show how corrupt our town council was, and she did that."

"Good," I say.

I hear a car door slam. We can't see the car from this point in the backyard, but there's no doubt who it is. I jump up from the table, Jenna close behind me.

As I come around toward the front, I see Brett. His smile is huge—he's nodding, and suddenly he's running at me and jumping into a huge hug. Jenna comes up from behind me and joins in.

The mayor clears her throat, and we all break apart.

"The congregation discussed, and your event is approved. June twelfth."

Ashley and Connor come up behind us.

"Good news?" Ashley asks.

I nod and smile. She grabs my hands and jumps up and down. "How much is the deposit? We've raised seven hundred and forty dollars so far, and—"

"No deposit," Mayor Miller says. "Spend that on decorations, or food, or whatever else you need."

The mayor walks confidently toward the backyard to spread the news to the adults.

"She paid for the deposit upfront," Brett says. "I don't know what that means about her feelings on all

245

this. I don't know if anything's changed. But I think that's a good thing."

I squeeze his shoulder. "That's a *very* good thing."

"Holy crap," Connor says. "We're really going to do this thing, aren't we?"

My gaze drifts up toward the barren flagpole.

"Hold on," I say. I sprint into the house, taking the stairs two at a time as I dash into my room, throw open my closet door, and see the colors shine back at me.

Back downstairs. Unfurled in my hand is the pride flag, slightly crumpled from its two-week stay in my closet.

"Let's raise this up," I say. "Together."

CHAPTER 32

In *Songbird Hollow*, my crops are all dried out. I forgot to water them one too many times, and they're unsalvageable. It's something I've never done in this game actually. I'd plan my whole weeks around my *Songbird Hollow* town, but over the last few weeks, I've been distracted, to say the least.

I take a tour of the town for sentimental reasons. I've got a feeling I won't be playing much more of this game for long. I've run out of side quests, my farm is huge, I've caught every fish, attended every party, seen every cutscene, befriended every villager, fallen in love, and married the digital love of my life.

I could keep growing my farm or wait for the developer to release an update. Or I could just wipe it all and start again. But *Songbird Hollow* filled this void I had in my life. This void that's not really there anymore.

When I walk into my *Songbird Hollow* farmhouse, I talk to Peter one last time. "Howdy, Jake," he says, like always, then follows up with a fact about his chickens. I gift him a hot pepper, and he glows with joy. A heart icon pops up, and he says, "My favorite! How did you know!" Even though I've given him a pepper every in-game day for the last two in-game years.

It's getting redundant. And that's okay. For once, I belong in another village.

I look to the window and see the flag waving in the wind. I'm still not sure I want to jump onto the Songbird Hollow message boards after everything that went down before, but I make a silent promise to post an update after the big event.

"McDonald's run?" Mom asks, peeking her head into my room. "We can drop food off at Dad's work on the way back."

"Sure, sounds good!"

When we get in the car, she lets me plug in my phone and play the music. I find a Spotify playlist, and the next thing I know, we're flying down the country roads, windows down, turning our arms into airplane wings.

"I was so worried about you when you came out to us," she says. "You know, I was watching that segment about that young boy who was the grand marshal of his pride parade, and I was tearing up, thinking about all the hate he must have gone through in his life. And how much more he'd have to deal with, just because of where he's from. I mean, even that interview might have gotten him a ton of hate."

"Oh," I say. "It made me cry for a completely different reason. I wanted to *be* him. He was so confident. Like being out and proud was just effortless. He was like a younger Jonathan Van Ness."

She laughs. "You're right. He was just like them."

"I just thought that could never be me. But now? I think it could." I sigh. "I'm sure I'll deal with more homophobes at some point in my life, maybe even at the pride festival, but I know I can handle it."

"I know you can handle it, too." She laughs. "And even if you can't, you have a great group of friends who will fight for you. Teachers, pastors, certain persistent candidates for mayor . . ."

"Plus you and Dad," I say.

She nods. "Okay, enough sentimental time. Let's go over logistics. I met with Susan again, and she's got all the usual food stands confirmed: lemonade, elephant ears, hot dogs, you get the picture."

"Ashley and her parents are using that money to buy as many pride hand fans, rainbow beads, bracelets, and headbands for all guests, and everything else we need."

"I talked with the band director, and though he said he can't add another mandatory event so late in the year, he is going to see if people will want to attend. He texted me right after class saying the whole drum-line already agreed, so we'll definitely have music, if a drumline counts as music."

"It counts," I say. "Jenna and I are creating pamphlets about the history of pride parades, riots, and festivals. We want people to be informed and as a bonus, Ms. Darcey said she'd give us both extra credit in history if we did a presentation in class."

Mom pulls to a stop outside Dad's factory, and he jumps into the car.

"Ah, McDonald's, awesome." He grabs the bag from us and starts eating, as the smell of metal and oil permeate the car. "What are we talking about?"

"How we were able to plan a whole festival in a matter of weeks," she says.

"Anything I can do to help?" Dad asks. "The whole

family is coming. Should I bring anything else?"

"There *is* one thing you can bring," I say.

He speaks between bites of food. "Oh, yeah? What's that?"

"Last time I was at the church, I noticed there was an old flagpole up there."

"Comically huge flags? That's my forte." Dad laughs. "Leave that to me."

CHAPTER 33

"Okay, done. What do you think?" Jenna asks.

Jenna's outfit is perfection. A rainbow tie-dyed crop top and bright pink pants. She's wearing her hair in a frizzy side pony with a silver scrunchie, and she's even gone the extra mile to die the tips of her hair blue. Her rainbow sunglasses complete the look.

"Too much?" she asks.

"For you, just enough," I say as I keep rooting through my closet.

"I told you to get a special shirt for this."

"I don't need one," I finally say. "Because I have this."

I pull out the red-and-black flannel shirt and quickly pull it on. With my tan shorts and rustic boots, it's kind of a look.

"It's . . . gay pride," she says. "Not lumberjack pride."

I roll my eyes. "Jenna, you don't get it. This is exactly what my character wears in *Songbird Hollow*. This is what I wore when I proposed to Peter."

Brett creeps into the room. "When you *what*?"

I sigh. "It's a video game thing. Forget I said anything."

"You look really cute," he says.

He's got a white tee on with a little rainbow flag on it. It's understated, and shy, but it looks nice on him.

"I know we shouldn't have trusted you from the start." Jenna groans. "Luckily, you've got a friend like me. Here—"

She passes out two more rainbow sunglasses, and we put them on and model them in my mirror.

"That will make up for whatever you two are doing fashion-wise."

"Ready to go?" Brett asks.

The three of us are in the back seat of the car as my parents drive us to the church. As we approach, we see a big group of our pep band classmates setting up their instruments.

Jenna gets out of the car and bounds over to them,

grabbing her cymbals from Connor, then throwing her arms around him in a tight hug.

"So, I guess she's not mad that Connor's science presentation got picked for that conference?" Brett asks.

"I guess not," I say with a light chuckle. "She must save all that competitive energy for you. Oh, hey, how'd your mom take it?"

"Not great at first. When she found out Ms. Nugent picked someone else, she thought there must be some mistake, and even said she was going to call the school and see if anything could be done about it." He sighs slowly, through his teeth. "I'm kind of glad she overreacted, though, because I was able to talk to her. Like, *really* talk to her about the pressure she's been putting on me."

"Oh, wow, you actually had the big talk! How did it go?"

"Surprisingly well," he says. "She got really sad, but we talked through it. She said she's been so worried about the election that she's been trying to control my grades. The town. Everything she can."

"I guess that makes sense," I say. "Doesn't make it okay, though."

"She told me to tell you she's sorry."

"Oh." I take a long pause.

"You don't have to accept it. I wasn't even going to tell you. But I think that's why she's been pitching in to help the church throw this." He shrugs. "At least she'll be off your back."

"Good," I say. "Maybe she'll have fun and realize how ridiculous she's been."

Dad goes to raise the flag in the center of the parking lot, while Mom goes to talk with the pastor, who's setting up cornhole boards and an outdoor seating area. Farther down the property, I see the line of food stalls getting ready, with Susan Lee popping in and out of each one.

Ashley comes up behind us, throwing rainbow beads over our heads and offering us first pick of all the goodies. I grab a rainbow bandanna, and Brett takes a handful of stickers; then she goes to set everything up in her area.

"It's almost time," Brett says as the band starts to warm up.

Since the parking lot is closed for the celebration, we can see cars start to line the streets, and people start pouring in from all directions. I feel my stress levels increasing with each person who walks in because it looks like a *lot* of people are going to hear my welcome speech.

But this time, my hands aren't shaking. I have a few note cards, but I'm just going to speak from the heart—and keep it short.

Brett comes up and starts to place pride stickers on my face. A rainbow on one cheek, an equality sign on the other. I start to laugh when I see the look of full concentration he's giving me.

"What?" he asks.

"Just thinking about that time I painted your face for the pep rally—before your mom yelled at me for giving you acne. It's funny. I didn't even know you like I do now, but . . . being this close to you made me want to lean in and kiss you."

He blushes, but he doesn't turn away. "Oh."

"I'm not going to," I say quickly. "Just saying that's a thing I might want to do someday. If you feel the same way."

There's a small pause. I feel so vulnerable, but I don't look away.

He nods. "Yeah, absolutely. Someday."

The band launches into the fight song, and it's like we're in a basketball game. Instead of the sea of red, it's a burst of every color. A rainbow of people weaving around us, toward the games, the food, the celebration.

It's everything I wanted. Everything *we* worked for.

When I look back to the church's rusty flagpole, I see that Uncle Jeremy's joined my dad to help hoist the flag. As the flag gets higher, people cheer louder. I run over and give them both a hug. My cousin Jess steps out from behind my uncle to reveal she's wearing a ridiculous rainbow wig.

"Best twelve dollars I've ever spent," she says, pointing at her hair. "Granny's going to hate it."

"Wait, *Granny's* coming?" I ask.

"Pretty much everyone's coming," Dad says.

"Not sure they'll all be following the strict rainbow dress code," Uncle Jeremy says with a laugh, "but they'll be here."

After posing for pictures with my family, they start to wander toward the main festivities, but I stand by the flagpole for a little bit longer. Soaking this all in.

Everything I love about Barton Springs is on display in front of me, and for once, I really do feel like I belong. And it's all because of this flag.

"You ready?" Brett asks, and I nod. Since we're somewhat alone here, he reaches for my hand and gives it a gentle squeeze, and we walk toward the stage. I know he's not ready to come out yet, but I can be patient. Like, digging-up-twenty-golden-seashells patient.

But he keeps his hand in mine as we push through the crowd. Just as the fight song ends, they play it again. The cymbals crash louder, the trumpets freer than in any basketball game I've ever been to.

Brett drops my hand, and I take the steps to the stage where a selection of local bands will be playing throughout the day. Mom gives me a thumbs-up from across the stage, where she's talking with the audio guy.

My nerves are in overdrive, but I feel more focused than ever as I approach the mic. The energy at the festival is electric, and I soak in as much of it as I can. The colors are so bright, and the crowd is growing by the minute. I clear my throat and grab the microphone, and I'm finally ready to make Barton Springs history.

Because this is Pride.

And we have a *whole* lot to celebrate.

EPILOGUE

Songbird Hollow Message Boards

Topic: Re: Small town pride

Post from: JakeyJake400

Hi friends,

It's been ages since I've been on here, it feels. But for good reason. I came back during BigotGate (I think that's what you all called it?) and seeing the hate speech all over this thread was kind of upsetting.

For those of you asking for an update, though, I have good news. I'm proud to announce that the village of Barton Springs, Ohio—population 2,023—successfully threw its first pride festival at the Barton Springs United Methodist Church.

More than a thousand people showed up, which is higher than so many of our other town festivals. So many people attended that the town hall had to bring it up in their monthly report—the village had never received such good press before, plus a bunch of business owners demanded we do this every year.

A few of you who seem to be from similar towns have asked for advice. I couldn't have done it without a ton of spontaneous support, plus a little bit of luck. But if you're thinking about starting your own pride parade, festival, picnic, or *whatever* in your town, I hope you can make it work.

And if not, there's always *Songbird Hollow*. Or, hey, make your way to Barton Springs next year.

Thanks for cheering me on from all over the internet. I'll see you all again when I do a replay.

Your friend and neighbor,
Jake

ACKNOWLEDGMENTS

After writing three young adult books, writing my first middle grade book was such a fun and exciting challenge. But I'll be honest: I couldn't have done it without the support of so many of you. Some thank-yous are in order:

To my agent, Brent Taylor, for his overwhelming support of my writing and for being an absolute expert in all things middle grade. I couldn't have done it without your tireless enthusiasm for this project.

To my wonderful editor, Megan Ilnitzki. From our very first call, you had such a strong vision for the project and I couldn't wait to execute it with your guidance. Also, to my entire team at HarperCollins for all their work to put this book in the hands of readers everywhere: Jacqueline Hornberger, Shona McCarthy, Mark Rifkin, Parrish Turner, KB Mello, Vincent Cusenza, Sean Cavanagh, Robert Imfeld, Emily Mannon, Patty Rosati, Mimi Rankin, Katie Dutton, and Anna Ravenelle.

To Violet Tobacco for bringing Jake to life in this brilliant and fun cover illustration, and to David E. Curtis for the incredible jacket design.

To Nic Stone, Claribel A. Ortega, Julie Murphy, and Maulik Pancholy for inspiring me to dip into the waters of middle grade books. To all my other writing friends for keeping my spirits high, boosting my books, and constantly reminding me why this is, hands down, the coolest profession in the world.

To my family across Ohio for constantly showing up for me with love and support over the years, especially when it came to my creative endeavors. From band shows to community theater plays to piano recitals—and now, to book launches—I'm so grateful that you always have my back.

And finally, to my husband, Jonathan, for everything you do to help me make my books the absolute best they can be. You're both my biggest cheerleader and strongest advocate, and I couldn't do it without you.